99%ありがとう
ALSにも奪えないもの　藤田正裕

99% THANK YOU...
THINGS EVEN ALS CAN'T TAKE AWAY
HIRO FUJITA

ポプラ社

もくじ CONTENTS

はじめに Introduction ·· 3

CHAPTER 1 ··· 23
0 〜 13 years old
Tokyo, New Jersey, Zurich, London
東京、ニュージャージー、チューリヒ、ロンドン

CHAPTER 2 ··· 41
13 〜 18 years old
Tokyo
東京

CHAPTER 3 ··· 57
18 〜 24 years old
Hawaii
ハワイ

CHAPTER 4 ··· 77
24 〜 30 years old
Tokyo
東京

CHAPTER 5 ··· 99
30 〜 XX years old
ALS
筋萎縮性側索硬化症

おわりに Acknowledgments ·· 206

カバー&扉写真
撮影　内田将二
撮影チーフ　千葉史郎・岡部雄二

ブックデザイン
長坂勇司

はじめに

Introduction

僕は今、
この文章を
目で書いている。

正確には、視線とまばたきで
パソコンを操作して書いている。
なぜなら、もうキーボードを
たたくことができないから。

僕は藤田正裕。
父の仕事の関係で海外での暮らしが長く、
みんなからは"ヒロ"と呼ばれている。

僕は、
ALS患者だ。

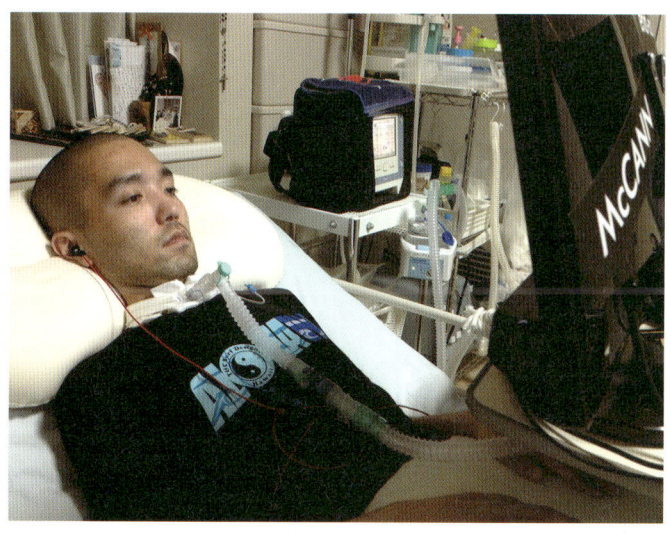

I'm writing these words with my eyes.
To be precise, I am working on a computer connected to an eye-tracking system.
This is how I operate my computer as I am no longer able to type or use the mouse.
My name is Masahiro Fujita.
I have lived abroad for many years due to my father's work.
People call me Hiro.
I have ALS. (also known as Lou Gehring's, or MND)

最初に言う。

これは「本」というより、僕の人生の短い「日記」。
ALS前と後の、ある日、ある出来事、ある思いを、
なるべく素直に記してある。
その瞬間によって、表情も言葉も違うであろう……。

幼少期から今まで、「普通」とは言えない恵まれた生活。
今はそれを取り戻す、貴重な闘いの経験をしている。

逃げることのできない現実。
日々、変わっていくさま。
生で共有させてください。

I'll tell you from the beginning.
This is not a book, but rather a short "diary" of my life.
Honest thoughts, emotions on certain days and happenings, before and after ALS.
I'm sure the "face" I show and my words vary psychotically.
Blessed with too good of a life since I was born.
And now, this precious experience, to fight and win it all back.
It's a reality I can't run from.
As "I" am changing every day, more dramatically than ever before.
Please let me share this "diary" as raw as I can.

僕はちゃんと生きた。

赤ちゃんのころは、
おばあちゃんにオムツを変えてもらっているとき、
おばあちゃんの顔にオシッコをかけた。

子どものころは、やんちゃで、
なにかあればサルみたいに高いところへ登って、
走り回って、怪我して、泣いて、また登った。

学生時代は、常に友達と遊び、スポーツ好きで、
恋愛好きで、酒好きで、イロイロ好きで、
少しは勉強もした。

I lived it...
When I was a baby, my grandma was changing my diapers and I surprised her by peeing on her face.
When I was small, I climbed anything like a monkey, ran around, got hurt, cried, and then climbed again.
When I was a student, I had too much fun hanging out with friends, playing sports, falling in and out of love, getting reeeaally drunk, etc...
I also studied a little along the way too.

社会人になると、ほとんどの先輩、
上司に叱られながら可愛がってもらい、
仕事を楽しみ、しっかり貢献もして、
会社を出たらまた16才に戻るような毎日だった。

楽しく、充実した、幸せな、恵まれた、日々を送り、
未来の計画、夢は大きく、たくさん持っていた……。

あのままなにもなければ、今ごろ、
奥さんと手をつないで
ベビーカーでも押してたかもね。

At work, I fought with and was scolded by my bosses and seniors a lot, but also got along with them really well. I enjoyed my work and did well for the company. Then when I stepped out of the office, I went back to being a teenager again. It was a good life.
My days were blessed with joy and happiness. I had big plans and dreams for the future…
Who knows, I might have been walking down the street with my wife and baby by now…

人生のす・べ・てが
変わった瞬間。

筋萎縮性側索硬化症(ALS)と宣告されたとき。
一瞬、狂った、喜怒哀楽のカクテル、
情緒不安定、めまい、悔しさの極限……。

2010年11月、検査入院していた病院の先生方に
丁寧にいろいろと説明してもらった。

だけど僕の耳に入ってきたのは、

In one moment, E-V-E-R-Y-T-H-I-N-G in my life changed...
I was diagnosed with Amyotrophic Lateral Sclerosis (ALS).
In that moment, a crazy cocktail of every emotion pierced through my body. It was, chaos, dizziness, and an unexplainable scale of frustration and anger…
It was November 2010. After a ton of tests, the doctors did their best to explain the diagnosis.
All I heard was:

「病名：筋萎縮なんとかなんとか。
あなたは、これからゆっくり動けなくなり、死ぬ。
余命は不明だが、長くはない。人それぞれ。
治療法はない。原因もわからない。希望もない。
人生お疲れでした」

ふざけんな……。

"The name of the disease is amyotrophic something something.
 You will gradually lose your ability to move and die.
 It's unclear how long you will live but it's not long… it depends on the patient.
 There is no cure. We don't know the cause.
 There is no hope.
 Thank you for playing."
Shhiiiiieeeeeett...

ALSとは、

終末期疾患（簡単にいうと、死に至る病）。

運動神経が攻撃され、全身麻痺を引き起こし、
肺にも致命的な影響を及ぼす。
少しずつ可動性を失っていく。
進行がゆっくりなため、体の異変になかなか気づかない。
皮膚の感覚や頭のなか（感覚神経と自律神経）は
これまでと変わらない。だから、これまでできたことは
そのままできると勘違いしてしまうし、
失敗するとふつうに痛い。

ALS is a terminal disease (simply put, it kills you).
It attacks the motor neurons leading to paralysis of the entire body and eventually fatally impacting the lungs.
It slowly robs you of your ability to move, but because it advances so slowly, it's difficult to detect the changes in your body.
Your sense of touch remains the same and your mind (sensory and autonomic nerves) is intact.
So it can fool you into thinking that you can do the usual.
Until you realize that you can't, and it just hurts.

For example, one day, you find that you can't brush your teeth or shave.
Or you suddenly collapse and break your front teeth.
Or somehow you find that you can't get up… stuck to your sofa.
Slowly, moving becomes a challenge.
Now, the only things I can move are my left index finger and my face…
Eventually, I will become a prisoner of my own body and will only be able to move my eyes.
But I believe… the eyes can still say a lot.

たとえば、なぜか歯みがきや、
髭剃りなどができなくなり、
なぜかなにもない場所で転ぶようになって
前歯を２本折ったり、
なぜか座り慣れているソファから
立ち上がれなくなる。
このように、毎日少しずつ体を動かすことが
困難になっていく。

**今では、動かせるのは
左の人差し指と顔だけ……。**

そして、僕はそのうち、体のなかに捕われ、
目しか動かせなくなるのだ。

**でも、きっと目だけでだって
たくさんのことが伝えられる。**

この病気の患者のなかには、
目の動きすら保障されていない人もいる。
それが自分であることが、僕の一番の恐怖だ。

それは
"TOTALLY LOCKED-IN STATE"
(完全に閉じこめられる)
と言われている。

Having said that, a small percentage of ALS patients aren't even guaranteed the movement of their eyes.
My greatest fear now is that I may be one of that small percentage…
It's pleasantly called the "TOTALLY LOCKED-IN STATE."

NOTHING moves… body, face, eyelids, eyeballs… nothing.
Completely cut off from the world…
A glass coffin, the body as your jail cell etc…
This is when I may give up.
So there IS a time limit…
I only hope I have the courage to overcome this challenge…

なにも動かない。体、肺、顔、目……なにも。
完全に一人、世と無関係。

でも頭のなかの僕は僕のまま。無限に考え続ける。
ガラスの棺おけ、自分の体の牢屋のなかで。

この状態になったら諦めるかも。
だから、タイムリミットはある。

どうかこれを
乗り越えられる
勇気が僕のなかに
あることを願う。

大勢の人と一緒に戦っている。

僕は今、家族、ヘルパー、看護師や医師、
多くの友達、会社の先輩・同僚たちに支えられて、
なんとか自分らしく生きている。

多くの理解ある人々のおかげで、
会社の仕事も続けられている。
会社には週一で出社して、
あとはメールで毎日やりとりしている。

I'm fighting this together with A LOT of people.
I'm able to live as close to "myself" as possible, thanks to the support of my family,
caretakers, nurses, doctors, many friends and colleagues.
Thanks to their support and understanding, I am able to keep working at the office as well.
I go to the office once a week and on other days I keep in contact via email.

ALSのことをもっと知ってもらい、
治療法の確立と患者の生活支援ができるよう、
「END ALS」という一般社団法人を立ち上げ
さまざまな活動を行っている。

http://end-als.com/

ALS発病後に始めたブログには、
直接知らない多くの人からも、
励ましの言葉をたくさんいただいている。

http://blog.honeyee.com/hfujita/
https://www.facebook.com/endalswithhiro

そして、海外でも「END ALS」の
活動は広がっている。

I also established an association called END ALS in order to help find a cure, build awareness, and provide support for ALS patients.
http://end-als.com/
I've received countless words of support from people through my blog which I started after I was ALS-ed.
http://blog.honeyee.com/hfujita/
https://www.facebook.com/endalswithhiro
The efforts of END ALS have gone abroad and growing.

ひとりでも多くの人に、
この病気について知ってもらいたい。
そのために、自分の人生をさらけ出すことが、
今の僕に与えられたミッション、
僕が選ばれた理由だと思っている。

正直、自分が発病する前は、
こんな残酷な病気のことは知らなかった。
いや、周りに情報はあったのかもしれないが、
自分とは無関係だと思っていた。

老若男女、誰でも、いつでもなりうるのに……。あなたも。

現に、今、日本には約9000人のALS患者がいる。

I want as many people as possible to know about this disease and help find a cure.
This is why I am exposing my life.
I think this is my mission…why I was chosen.
Honestly, I never imagined that such an evil disease existed.
Actually, there probably was information around but I just didn't think that it was relevant to me.
Now I know it can happen to anyone, at any time regardless of age or gender. Yup, even you.
In fact, there are roughly 9000 randomly chosen patients in Japan today, and growing.

この病との戦いはもう３年半。
勝ち目のない喧嘩を売られた。
でも、負けるわけにはいかない
理由が多すぎる。だから戦う。

そして
絶対勝つ。

It's been three and a half years since my fight with ALS began.
I've been picked a fight that can't be won.
But I have too many reasons why I can't lose.
So I guess I'm just going to have to win...

99%ありがとう

「家族」、いつも好き勝手やらせてくれてありがとう。
けど、俺が守ってあげるはずなのに、
できなくてごめん……。

「友達」、愛と勇気、生きる理由をくれてありがとう。
けど、会うたび、恋しすぎて、つらい……。

「会社」、社会とのつながり、
自分の存在意義を作ってくれてありがとう。
けど、昔ほど「貢献」できなくて、
いつも悔しい……。

「ヘルパー・看護師・医師」、
この小さな命をつなげてくれてありがとう。
けど、失礼ながら皆様に頼らなくていい日を、
毎日、夢見てる……。

「研究者」、世界の最前線での実績、ありがとう。
けど、一日でも早く、ALS患者へのiPS医療の治験を
実行してください……。

「政府」、保険制度などの努力をありがとう。
けど、一日でも早く、ALS患者へのiPS医療の治験を
許可して援助してください……。

「ALS」、初心、物事の真の価値を教えてくれて、ありがとう。
けど、オマエには死んでもらう……。

" 99% Thank You"...

"My family," thank you for always letting me live as I want.
I know that it's my turn to help you… but I can't… I'm sorry…
"My friends," thank you for giving me the love, courage, and reason to live.
But every time I see you…I wish I had more time together, it hurts…
"My work," thank you for keeping me connected to society and adding to my reason to be.
But because I can't contribute as I have in the past, I'm left with guilt and frustration all the time…
"My caretakers, nurses, and doctors," thank you for connecting this small life.
No disrespect, but e-v-e-r-y-d-a-y I dream of the day when I won't have to rely on you.
"Researchers," thank you for raising the bar at the forefront of research globally.
But please conduct iPS stem cell based clinical trials on ALS patients as soon as possible.
"Government," thank you for your efforts to improve insurance policies, etc.
But please allow and fund iPS stem cell based clinical trials on ALS patients as soon as possible.
"ALS," thank you for reminding me the essence, the true value of life.
But I'm going to have to kill you…

CHAPTER 1

0〜13 years old

Tokyo, New Jersey, Zurich, London
**東京、ニュージャージー、
チューリヒ、ロンドン**

畳が懐かしい

1979年11月、東京の経堂で生まれた。
親の仕事の関係で、3か月後にはアメリカのニュージャージーに、
5歳からはスイスのチューリヒに、
さらに7歳からはイギリスのロンドンに6年住んだ。

6歳上の兄(まーちゃん)と話すときは英語。親とは日本語。
友達とは9:1で英語。
日本語は話すことはできたが、読み書きはほとんどできなかった。

当時、日本にはときどき夏休みに帰国していたくらい。
自分にとっては完全に異国・謎・不思議な国だった。
けど一度、帰国中に畳屋の前を通ったとき、幼いながら、
なぜか「懐かしい」と心地よさを感じたのを覚えている……。

The Tatami DNA
I was born in Kyodo, Tokyo in November 1979.
Due to my father's work, we moved to New Jersey, the U.S. when I was 3 months old, then to Zurich, Switzerland at age 5. At age 7, we moved to London, the U.K., and lived there for 6 years.
I spoke English with my brother, Ma-chan, who is 6 years older, and Japanese with my parents. I spoke mostly English with my friends. Back then, I could speak Japanese but could hardly read or write.
We would occasionally go back to Japan during our summer breaks.
To me, my so called home, Japan was so mysterious and very foreign.
But somehow, on one of our trips back, we passed by a *Tatami* store, and I distinctly remember stopping and feeling so comfortable, or even a sense of nostalgia…

イグルー

ニュージャージーにいたころのある日、
雪が1メートルぐらい積もっていた。

兄の友達たちが遊びに来て、イグルー（かまくら）を作ったらしい。
小学生にもなっていない僕は持ち上げられ、
そのイグルーのテッペンに投げられた。
イグルーはもちろん崩れ、僕は逆さまに雪に埋もれた。

知ってました？　埋もれているときって、
どっちが上かわからないの。
さすがに数分たったら兄たちも焦ったようで、
掘って足からつり出された。
初めて死ぬかと思った。
初めて殺そうかなとも思った（笑）。

The igloo
One cold day in New Jersey, about a meter of snow fell.
My brother's friends were over at the house and they made an igloo.
I was still in preschool. They decided to pick me up and throw me on top of it.
Naturally, the igloo crumbled and I was literally buried, upside down.
Did you know that when you are buried you can't tell which way is up?
As I didn't/couldn't move for few minutes, the guys started to panic and pulled me up, by my feet.
It was the first time I thought I might die…
Ironically, it was also the first time I thought of killing someone too…

「助けて！」

スイスではインターナショナルスクールに通ってた。
校庭がすごく広かった。
ある日、休み時間になにをしようかなと考えていた。
中学生のなかで兄はサッカーをしていた。
そこに入るわけにはいかないし……。

小学２、３年生は砂場で山を作っていてつまらなそうだったので、
同学年の１年生と鬼ごっこをした。

すると、大失敗。夢中で逃げていたら、やっちまった。
２、３年生が作っていたつまらない山を踏んで潰してしまった。
そしたら５、６人に囲まれボコボコに……。

小２レベルなのでたいしたことなかったけど、怖くて、逃げた。

"Help!"

In Switzerland, we went to an international school with a huge school yard.
One day, I was thinking of what to do during recess.
My brother, who was already in junior high, was playing soccer with the big boys.
I thought to myself, "I can't join them."
The second and third graders were making a mountain in the sandbox and that looked boring so I joined the game of tag with my first grade classmates.
As I was running around like crazy I accidentally stepped on the stupid mountain that the second and third graders were making.
Suddenly, I was surrounded and was being pushed and punched around…
It wasn't that serious as they were second graders but it was scary enough, I ran.

「まーちゃん！　助けて！　鬼ごっこして、走ってたら……」

兄に全部説明した。すると半ギレの兄が、

「自分でどうにかしろ」

って、サッカーに戻っていった。
…………。

りょーかい。

"Ma-chan! Help! We were playing tag and I was running and…"

I explained the whole story to my brother and he just stood there looking pissed, and said,
" Take care of it yourself"
and went back to his soccer game…
RRRiiiiiiight...
Ok...

一生の付き合い

インターナショナルスクールの子は、一見バラバラに見えるが、
行動範囲が似ているのか、同じ「人種」が少ないからなのか、
大抵一生の付き合いになっている。

ニュージャージーで親どうし仲のいい家族がいて、
そこのお嬢様と３、４歳のころ、二人で「結婚する〜」とか言ってた。
するとその事実を知らずに、
高校時代に彼女と日本で再会し、付き合うことになった。

小２のころ、イギリスで同じクラスで、
よくケンカもしつつ仲の良かった友達が、
日本のアメリカンスクールの高校でまた一緒になった。
そういうことがあると、兄弟的な感情がわく。

**だから「一期一会」という言葉があるけど、
僕は「一期多会」の精神で人と付き合うことが多い。**

Friends for life

Kids at international schools may look like a diverse bunch but because we tend to move around in the same circle or because we are simply a group of "minorities," for the most part, we end up being friends for life.

For example, in New Jersey, when I was 3 or 4, we had a close family friend. I often played with their daughter and we ran around saying, "We're going to get married!" Then I started to date a girl in high school. A few months in our relationship, we found out… she was that same girl from Jersey! We had no idea.

Or, when I was in second grade in the U.K., there was a friend from the same class who I played and fought with a lot. We became classmates once again in high school in Japan. Things like this lead to a sense of brotherhood.

There is a saying in Japanese that roughly translates to," treasure every encounter, as if it's a once in a lifetime experience" but I tend to engage in relationships with an attitude to" treasure every encounter, as if you will meet again."

今、この瞬間

ヨーロッパのほとんどの場所へ家族旅行で行った。
小学生ながら、景色を見て「すげー……」と思ったのを覚えている。

ギリシャの青い海をバックにした遺跡とオリーブの木、
ベネチアのテーマパーク感、
スコットランドで夜に見えた永遠に続く丘、
スイスの山々のふもとにあるおもちゃみたいな村や、
頂上からの景色などが特に衝撃的だった。

**まさに今、この瞬間も、そこで生活している人々や
喜怒哀楽が存在していると思うとワクワクするし、
いい意味で自分の愚かさを感じる。**

いつか、自分の奥さんと子どもと
同じ景色を見るのが目標になっていった。

At this very moment…
As a family, we travelled to most parts of Europe.
I remember, even as a young boy, being amazed with the scenery.
The ruins and the olive trees with the beautiful blue Greek ocean in the background,
The theme park-like wonders of Venice,
The ever-rolling green hills of Scotland at night,
The toy-like villages at the foot of the Swiss mountains,
The sight from the top has especially stuck with me my whole life.
**Even today, when I think of the people of those places, their lives, their joys and sorrows that exist at this very moment, that's exciting.
It's humbling.**
Somewhere along the way,
I was hoping to enjoy the same scenery and feelings with a family of my own someday…

草サッカー

イギリスの公園はとにかく広く、芝生が多い。
必ず、草サッカーをやっているグループがいくつもいた。
フルコートからミニゲーム、大人から子どもまで。
小学生のころはよく参加した。

イギリスのアメリカンスクールではうまいほうだったが、
現地の子たちとやると圧倒されっぱなし。
技術とかじゃなくて、気合、負けず嫌い、
「自分がスターだ」という気持ちの差だった。

小3くらいでも、シャツは引っ張る、押す、削りに来る。
そのうち慣れて、それが楽しくなった。
高校では、自分も相手の脇腹に右フックを入れたりしてた……(笑)。

フェアプレーでも体入れでは負けなかった。
167センチ、65キロの自分が、
でっかい外人相手に負けなかったのは
"気持ち"だけだったと思う。

Pick up games

The great thing about the U.K. is that their parks are huge and grassy. There were always groups of soccer games here and there, from full pitch to mini games, from adults to kids.
In my elementary school years, I often took part in these games.
I was one of the better players at the American School in London but when I played with the locals, I was always blown away.
It's not that they had better technique.
It was their determination to not lose, their intensity, their hunger, their self-belief that they are the star.
At 3rd grade, they pull your shirt, push you, and tackle your legs.
Soon I got used to this intensity and enjoyed it.
By the time I was in high school, I was giving right hooks to the kidney….
Even in a fair game, I was never overpowered by the body checks.
At 167cm-tall and at 65kg,
the only reason I didn't lose against big-ass non-Japanese was, intensity.

初彼女

小２のころ、メガンって子と付き合った。
小２だから恋愛というより、単なるステータス感だったと思う。

電話で告白して、OKをもらった。

**電話を切ったら、
知らないうちに
飛び跳ねて拳を振り上げ
「YES!!」だって……。**

誰も見てなかったけど恥ずかしかった。

First girlfriend
In 2nd grade, I went out with a girl named Megan.
At that age, it wasn't really romance but more about status.
I called her on the phone, asked her out and she said yes.
When I hung up, I jumped with my fist in the air and yelled "She said YES!!!!"
No one was watching, but it was still really embarrasing.

勉強

小学生のころ、平日はアメリカンスクールに通い、
毎週土曜に日本語の補習校へ行った。
その日本語の宿題がイヤでしょうがなかった。

ある日、親が兄を迎えに行く間、
「ヒロは漢字をここまでやっときなさい」と……。

絶対イヤだ。
いろんな言い訳を考えたが、全部すでに使用済みだった。
なぜか「骨折るしかねー」と、思った。

2階の階段から落ちてみた。けど、ちょ――痛いだけ。
腕をソファとソファの肘置きに乗せて踏んで、膝蹴り入れてみた。
ちょ――痛いだけ。

そんなことをやっているうちに親が帰ってきた！
ヤバイ、どうしよう……どうしよう…………。

もしかして、ここは逆に……

「ちょっと外で遊んでくるー」

そしたら、「はーい」だって！

ハハハッヒヒヒッホホホッ。「はーい」だって！

そして私は遊んだのだ。

Study
During elementary school, I went to the American school during the week and to a Japanese school on Saturdays.
And I HATED the homework from that Saturday school.
One day, when mom was about to leave to pick up my brother, she said,
"Hiro, you work on the kanji up to here while I'm out."
Heeeell no…
I tried to find an excuse but realized that I had used them all.
For some reason, the only option I thought of was "I have to break my arm."
I tried everything. From falling down the stairs from the second floor but it just hurt like hell. Nothing broke.
Next, I put my arm on the armrest of two sofas, and stepped on it, kneed it but it just hurt like hell. Nothing broke.
Soon, my mom came home!
Shoot! What to do!? What to do…
Wait… what if I try the opposite?
I said "I'm going out to play for a bit!"
And what do you know, she said,"OK~."
Buhahaha! Yeeeuuup!
She said," OK~."
hahaha
And so, I played on.

教え

親から、
「人に迷惑掛けるな」
「男はトイレで泣け」
「左様心得よ」

兄から、
「人につばは吐くな」
「人の手紙は読むな」
「自分が同意するアドバイスだけ聞け」

パッと思い出せる
小学校時代の家族からの教え。

兄のしか守ってない（笑）。

Teachings
From my parents:
"Don't burden others!"
"Men never cry in public."
"Know your place." (some old samurai saying)
From my brother:
"Don't spit on others."
"Don't read other people's letters."
"Only listen to advice that you agree with."
Just some of the family moral lessons that comes to mind.
Come to think of it, I've only followed my brother's.

6歳差

生まれたころから、サッカー・レスリング・チェス・競走、
すべての対戦相手は6歳上の兄・まーちゃん。

幼少時代の6歳差は大きい。
けど、負けると悔しくてたまらなかった。常に本気でぶつかってた。
わざと勝たせてくれたりした日にはぶち切れて、終わらせなかった。

おかげでその後、同級生や体の大きい外国人と対戦するときには、
事前にズルの仕方や技を相当研究した上で挑めた。

6 year difference
Since I was born, whether it's soccer, wrestling, chess, or running, my first and biggest rival was Ma-chan.
A six year difference is huge when you're small.
Regardless, I was furious every time I lost. I always went at him all out.
If he even dared to let me win, I went crazy and didn't let the game be over.

However, thanks to this, I had years of practice and was ready by the time I had to take on my classmates or non-Japanese who were always much bigger than me.

勝負

まーちゃんと最後にサッカーの1対1をやったのは、
15年ぐらい前かな。

二人とも本気で1時間ぐらい体をぶつけ合い、削り合って、
二人の世界に没頭した。

一言も話さなかった。

まるで病気になるって知っていたかのように……。

同点だった。

気持ちよかった……。

The last battle

The last time Ma-chan and I played one-on-one in soccer was about 15 years ago.
For an hour, we completely zoned-in our own world, with all the body checks, pushing and pulling.
No words.
As though we knew that I was going to get sick...
It was a tie...
It felt good...

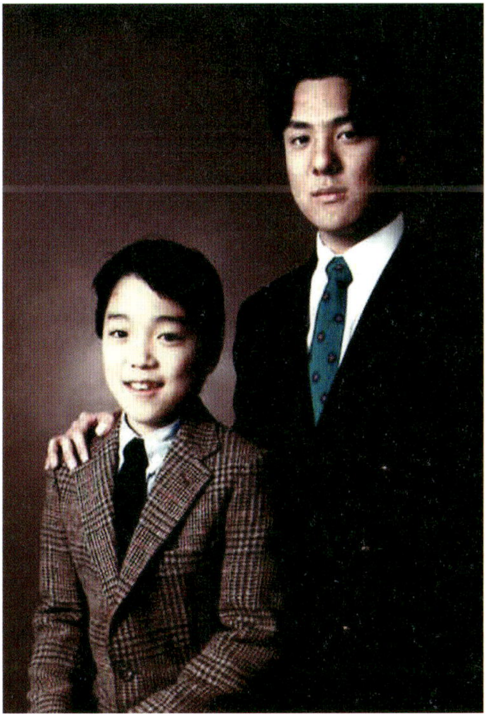

CHAPTER 2

13〜18 years old

Tokyo
東京

ん？　日本？

13歳のとき、イギリスから日本に帰国。
お茶の水女子大学附属中学校に編入した。

ん？
なんか懐かしいけど、なにかがすごい変……。

制服、寝ぐせ、規則だらけ、すべて選択されてる。
道が狭い、公園は泥、タクシーのドアは自動。
なんじゃ満員電車、人種が少ない、みんな同じ……。

で、なんでゴミ箱を電柱の上に置いてるの？

わけわからん……

Japan?
At age 13, we moved back to Japan from the U.K.
My new school was the Junior High School of Ochanomizu University.
It was nostalgic but at the same time it was really weird.
School uniforms, bed hair, a lot of regulations, not many options.
Narrow roads, parks with dirt grounds, automatic taxi doors...
Crazy packed trains, everybody the same race, everybody the same...
And what's up with the garbage bins above the electricity poles?
What is this place?

友達の名前が読めん！

「大石」が記号にしか見えなかった。
「☆□」にしか見えなかった……。

Can't read her name.
The Japanese *kanji* "大石" looked like "☆□".

日本で初の一生の仲間

日本に慣れるまでに救ってくれたのは、
やっぱりいろいろ言いあった仲間。

よくケンカしあった、いじめあった、
ウソつきあった、助けあった、仲間。

彼らが日本を教えてくれた。
20年経っても、必ず月一は一緒に飲んでたな……。
家族だね。いつでも命を預けるし預かる。

幸せ者です。

My first friends for life in Japan
What saved me from all the confusion and helped me to find my place were my friends I had some pretty intense moments with.
We fought, lied, bullied, laughed and helped each other.
They introduced Japan to me.
Twenty years later, we would still meet up for drinks, at least once a month.
My fam. I would give my life for them, and they'd do the same for me.
I am truly blessed.

Our soccer team & Nabe-san
During my junior high school days, after lunch, the only thing on my mind was after school sports.
We were hardly a contender but it was fun.
Our field was dirt… but we practiced freely until it was dark.
Our coach was nice but also scary, depending on the day.
His name was Mr. Watanabe. We called him Nabe-san.
During matches, he was the type to be yelling at us while smoking 2 packs of cigarettes.
He passed away four years ago due to subarachnoid hemorrhage.
Before he passed away I had the chance to visit him alone at night at his hospital.
I entered the dark room and found Nabe-san, looking skinny and weak.

サッカー部、ナベさん

中学時代は、午後になると部活のことしか考えてなかった。
チームはかなり弱かったけど、楽しかった。
砂みたいな土のグラウンドで、暗くなるまで自由に練習した。

監督は、ときに優しく、ときにはメチャ怖い、
渡辺先生ことナベさん。
試合のときは、ベンチでタバコを2箱ぐらい吸いながら怒鳴ってた。

4年ほど前に、クモ膜下出血で亡くなった。

亡くなる前、仕事の都合で、親族もいない夕方に一人で見舞いに行った。
そこには、弱ってるナベさんが寝ていた。

声をかけると、目を開けて、視線が合った。

「藤田だよ」

って言うと、苦しそうに涙を流した。
1分後、また寝た。

僕は凍ったまま……。動けなかった。悔しかった。

数年後、自分が似た立場で闘うとは……。

絶対ナベさんは「もっと行け！」って怒鳴ってくれてると思う。

I called out to him; he opened his eyes, our eyes met.
"Hey, it's me, Fujita."
I saw the pain and tears rolled down his face.
Then, a minute later, he fell back asleep.
I froze… I couldn't move. It really enraged, and frightened me.
Who would've thought that I would be fighting a similar fight now…
I can imagine Nabe-san yelling, "C'mon, you can do it!"

0点？
人生にぜんぜん関係ない

日本語がわからない。問題が読めない。
おかげで中間・期末は0点、1点、2点を集めてた。

「14世紀に△△△を□□□□にしたのは？」

ん〜、「ビートたけし」みたいな……知るかっ。

英語は100点とれてたけど、
さすがに「ヤバイ」ってちょっと思ってた。

実際は、人生においてホントにどうでもよかった。
先がどうなるかわかる計算なんてない。
なるようになる。

学ぶなら生き方の「アドリブ力」の授業が必要だと思う。

0 on tests? It really didn't matter
I didn't know much Japanese. I couldn't read the problems in the tests.
My scores for the mid-term and term exams were 0s, 1s, and 2s.
"In the 14th century, △△△ discovered □□□□ ?"
Um, "Brad Pitt…?" How the hell am I supposed to know?!
I got 100s on English but it was safe to say that I was in a bit of trouble to find a Japanese high school that will accept me.
However, as it turned out, it really wasn't that important in my life.
There is no formula that tells you what happens in the future.
Life will take its own course.
If we ARE to study, we need classes on how to "improvise" more than anything.

アメスク入学

最初から諦めていた高校受験は、もちろん失敗。
「この状況だと都内で入れる学校は一校しかない」と言われた。
「それならば」ということで、親は日本の学校は諦め、
僕は念願のアメリカンスクールに戻れることになった。

成績が悪すぎて、第一志望に行くことになった。

何か面白いでしょ。

The American School In Japan
I didn't have any faith in my results for the entrance exams for high school. And I was right.
I was told that, "With these grades there is maybe one school that you can get into in all of Tokyo."
Well, if the level of school is THAT low, my parents thought it might be better to take a different route.
I won my ticket back to American school.
My grades were so bad that I ended up with my first choice.
An interesting twist of fate.

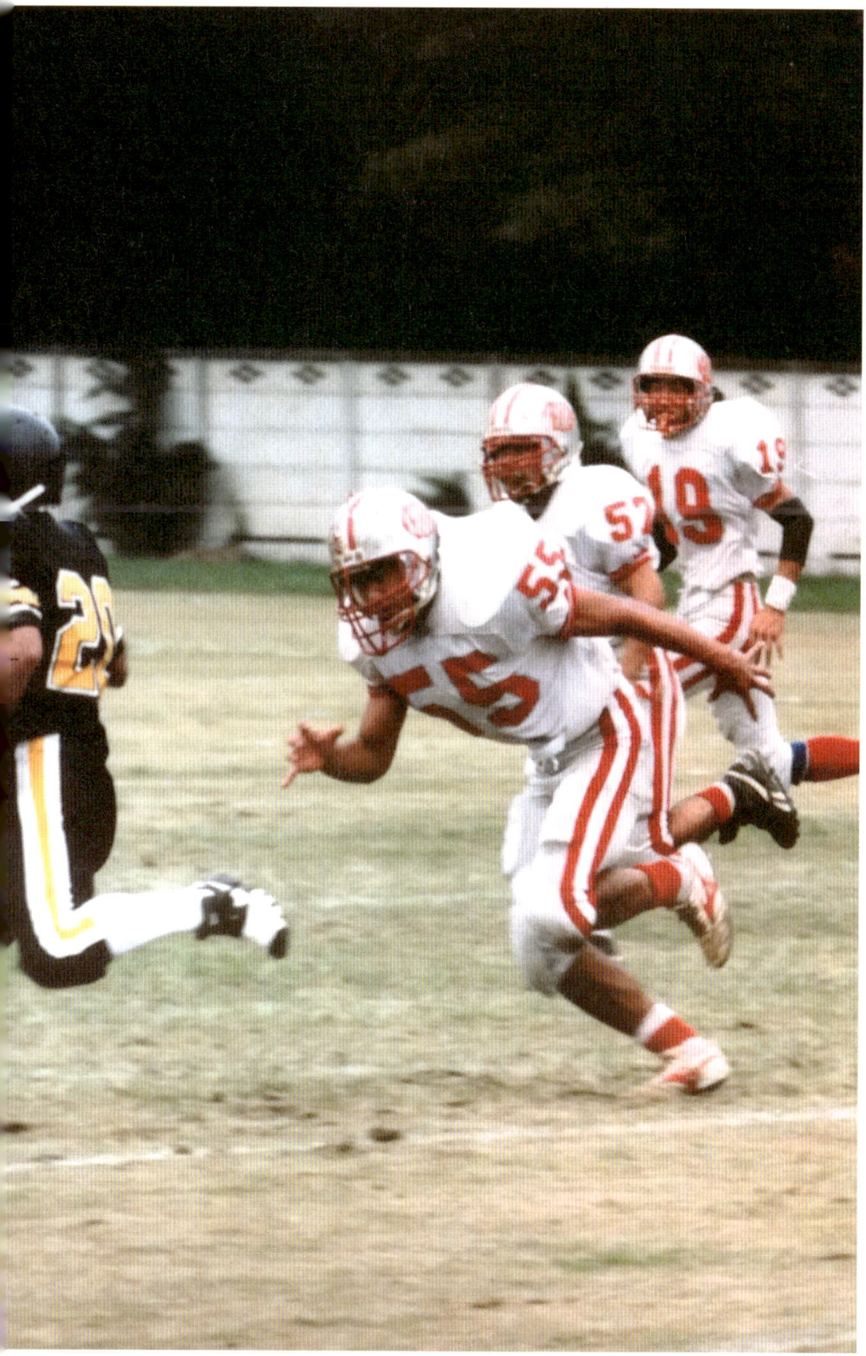
55
57
19

強かった、オレ

アメリカンスクールやアメリカでは、
1年に3つ部活をやることになっている。
僕はサッカー、陸上、アメフトをやっていた。
部活の対戦相手はすべてアメリカ軍基地の高校。

あるアメフトの試合では、相手が全員覚醒してた。
明らかに、なにか打ってた……。

違う試合では、ヘルメットのマスクをヤスリで尖らせていた。
腕がサクッと切れた。けど勝った。
ボケが……。

サッカー、陸上、アメフト、
すべてMVP、選抜、キャプテン。
一応、体だけは丈夫だった。

正直、自分は無敵だと思っていた。ホントに恥ずかしいほど、愚かだった。

Invincible…
At the American school, you can participate in 3 sports clubs per year. We always played against the U.S. military base schools. In one of the football matches, the entire opposing team was high on something. Clearly, they had shot up before the game. In a different game, they had their helmet mask sharpened and it slit my arm, a clean cut.
We still won though. Jack ass…
Soccer, Track, American Football, I was the MVP, All Star, captain in everything. I used to have a pretty tough body… **Back then, I thought that I was invincible. What a fool I was…**

オレってなに者？

アメスクで同じ人種に会えた。
日本と外国の間に挟まれて、生きている人たち。

英語も日本語もちゃんぽん。
ときには日本人以上に日本人。
ときにはアメリカ人以上にアメリカ人。
ただ、変なこだわりはなく、自由に生きてる。

この時期、よく葛藤があった。
国籍はあるけど「態度」が違うからって受け入れてくれない日本人。
態度もなんでも受け入れてくれるけど、
国籍はもらえないアメリカ。自分はなに人？　なに者？

けど、ここでも同じ悩みを持つ一生の仲間に出会えた。
やっぱり幸せ者だ。

What am I?

At the American school, I met people "like me," people who live between Japan and another country.
We speak a mixture of English and Japanese.
At times we're more Japanese than the Japanese, and more American than the Americans.
We just lived freely without any preconceived notions on things.
Back then, I was often very torn inside.
I'm a Japanese national but socially not accepted because of how I behave.
I'm socially perceived as an American but no citizenship from the States.
What am I? Who am I?
But luckily, I was able to meet friends who shared similar dilemmas.
Again, my friends for life.
I am blessed to have found them.

怪我をしない方法

アメフトでいろいろ学んだ。
なかでも、怪我をしない方法。
僕はたぶん、どのチームでも一番身体が小さかった。
スピードを買われていただけ。
始めた当初は、倍以上あるバカでかい相手とぶつかるのが
痛かったし、怖かった。
そのため、力を抜いて練習や試合をしていたら、監督は激怒。
「怪我するぞ！」と。
「は？　強いのに強く当たったらもっと痛いじゃん」
と思ったが、違った！
思いっきりぶつかったほうが痛くないし、
重心が低い分、向こうが吹っ飛んだりした。
なんでもそうやね。

思いっきり
ぶつかったほうが、
失敗しても痛くない。

How not to get hurt
I learned a lot through American Football. In particular, a way not to get injured or hurt. I was probably the smallest one in the league. All I had was speed. When I first started, I was scared shitless about tackling someone twice my size and it hurt like hell too! So, I practiced with half my strength. The coach knew it and he let me have it. "You're gonna get hurt!" I said, "Huh? If two forces run into each other harder, logically thinking, it would hurt even more." I was wrong. It hurts less if you go at them with your full strength, and taking advantage of my low center of gravity, sometimes I was able to put them on their ass. I guess this can be said for anything in life. **If you go at it with all you've got, even if you fail, it won't hurt as much.**

自信過剰

この時期の自分は、過剰な自信を持っていた。
そのおかげで、なにかイヤなことや「最悪の事態」が起きても、

「自分は耐えられるから
×××が起きたんだ」

と、勝手に思い込んでた。

今、その気持ちを懸命に
思い出そうとしている。

Overconfident

Back then, I remember being extremely overconfident.
Because of this, when something bad happened, I was able to fool myself that "This only happened to me because I can take it."
Now, I'm desperately trying to remember that mindset.

仲間

高校時代の15、16歳あたり、自分より背の高い、
金髪で瞳が緑の彼女がいた。
1年近く続いた。

週4、5くらいで彼女の家に泊まっていた。
友達とも学校でしか会わなかった。
友達たちが彼女の家まで、「六本木行こうや」と
誘いに来たこともあったけど、断ってた。

かなり惚れこんでた。
けど、別れることになった。

「やべー、ノコノコ戻っても友達は受け入れてくれないなー」
と、思った。
だけど、誰一人、一言も、イヤミも冗談も言わず、以前と一緒。

感動した。

人は、ときには自分の道を探し求めるため、
仲間を離れることがある。

そういうとき、「なんだよあいつ」「付き合い悪いな」
「変わった」って言う人もいる。

けど、本当の仲間は、そいつの気が済んで振り返るときまで待って、笑顔で迎えてくれる。

たとえそれが、数年後でも。
それができない男には「仲間」とか語ってほしくない。

Friend, boy, brother, sister...
When I was 15, 16, I was dating a beautiful blond, green-eyed girl, who was taller than me. We dated for about a year. During this time I would stay over at her house 4 or 5 times a week! I only met my friends at school. They would come over to her house to try and get me to go out to Roppongi with them. I never did. Yes, that's correct. I was whipped! (in love) But eventually we broke up. I thought, "Damn, my friends probably won't want to hang with me anymore after I ignored them for so long…" But nobody said a thing about it. No jokes, no sarcasm. Simply back to how it was. It was a pretty emotional moment for me… For various reasons, sometimes, we part ways with our friends to find our own. That's life, it's inevitable. Some friends will say, "What's up with him?!" or "he's changed," "fuck him" and move on. **But a true friend will be there with a smile, when you turn around after you're satisfied and done with whatever you needed to do…** Even if that takes years. If you don't feel this, don't use the terms friend, boy, brother or sister so lightly.

CHAPTER 3
18〜24 years old

Hawaii
ハワイ

ハワイの仲間

高校で仲の良かった友達数人が、ハワイの大学へ進学を決めていた。
いろんな意味で、日本とアメリカの間ってことで、
半年間、ロサンゼルスで遊んで（？）から僕もそうした。

先にハワイに行っていた友達が、現地で新しい仲間を作って
待っていてくれた。
正直、ほぼ全員なにかしら違法だった。
想像できる悪さはすべて、誰かがやってた。

だけど、当時はなぜかそういう人たちと肌が合った。

「ハワイにも外は違っても、
中身が素直でいい奴らがたくさんいるんだ……」

と、なんとなく嬉しかったのを覚えてる。

一生の仲間がまた増えた。

Friends from Hawaii

A few of my close friends from high school went to Hawaii for college.
And in many ways, Hawaii is between Japan and the U.S.
So, I decided to transfer there too after half a year of "partying" in LA.
My friends from Tokyo had already made a group of local friends and I was able to just jump in.
It's funny now to think almost everybody was doing something illegal.
Whatever you can imagine, somebody was/is doing it.
But somehow, those were the guys we got along with.
I remember being glad thinking,
"These guys are honest and have their own principles they live by, even though they may look crazy and wild... (and ugly, I joke, I joke ☺) on the outside."
Another group of friends for life.

差別、平等、いじり

昔から、どちらかというと毒舌と言われるほうだった。
これもハワイが自分に合った理由かもしれない。

アメリカのハワイ以外の州では、
「お互いの違いはない」を原則に、平等を尊重するように見える。

ハワイでは、ほとんどの人がミックスだ。
16分の1フィリピン人、16分の1日本人、16分の1ハワイ人、
韓国人、中国人、ポルトガル人、などなど……。

ハワイでは「みんな違う」。
お互いの違いをいじり、笑い合い、平等を尊重する。
それがすごく性格に合った。

正直にお互いの違いを認めて笑い合えてこそ、本当の平等があると思う。

国連のコンセプトでもいいぐらいだ。

Discrimination, Equality, Make fun

I've always been known to be more on the blunt side.
This may be why I felt at home in Hawaii.
To me, it seems like more people from other states in the U.S. value equality based on the notion that we are all the same, that there is no difference between you and I.
But in Hawaii, the majority of the people are mixed.
1/16 Filipino, 1/16 Japanese, 1/16 Hawaiian, Korean, Chinese, Portuguese, etc.
In Hawaii, "everybody IS different."
We point out the differences, joke and laugh about it all the time and that's how equality is respected.
This really fit my personality.
True equality can only exist when we can accept our differences and laugh about it. This should even be the concept for the U.N.

無理するな

波がでかく、潮の流れの強いポイントがあった。
しかも、波はビーチから数十メートルしか離れていないので、
地面に叩きつけられ、首を折る人もいる。
現地の友達も入らない、入れないこともよくあった。

そこに入ることが、いつの間にか自分のなかで肝試しになっていた。

ある日、友達たちも
「今日は止めとく」と言うなか、
入ることにした。
「もういいや、オレ」って。

Don't push it

There's a beach with huge waves with a strong current called Sandy beach.
Plus, the waves break really close to shore, so it's not uncommon to hear of people breaking their neck. There were many times when even my local friends wouldn't/couldn't go into the water too.
AND I'm not a great swimmer.
It became a serious dare for me...
One day, when my friends all said," no, not today,"
I decided to go in. " Fuck it"

入った瞬間、「やべっ、今日は間違ったかも」と思い、
15分ぐらいずっと、陸に戻ろうと大波を潜りながら、
がむしゃらに泳いだ。
友達かライフガードを呼ぼうとしたが、聞こえるはずがない。

「これは死ぬかも」 と思いながら、
海にいるロコに、

「助けて！ どうすれば戻れる!?」
って懸命に聞くと、

「とりあえず落ち着け」 と言い、
あのヤロー目を合わせながらゆ〜っくりと離れて行った。
そりゃそうだよね……。

溺れそうだったので、
もう首を折ってでも
次の大きい波に乗って陸に戻ろうと、

覚悟を決めた。

戻れた……。
嬉しく、大の字になって笑った。

友達のところへ戻ったら、レゲエ音楽をかけ、
皆で飲んで楽しい時間を……。

「おい！」って怒鳴ったら、
「えっ？　どうした〜？」だと。

From the moment I stepped in, I knew I made the wrong decision,"Daaaaaaamn Hiro..."
For the next 15 minutes, I was swimming like crazy trying to get out while ducking waves.
I yelled out to my friends and lifeguards but obviously they couldn't hear me.
Thinking,**" I'm gonna die,"** I called out to a local "bradah" in the water, **" Help me, how do I get out !?"**
He said,**" Calm down brah."**
Then the fucker kept an eye on me and slowly drifted away.
Well, I guess that's the smart thing to do.
I was really about to drown so I decided to risk breaking my neck and catch the next big one and try to get back to shore.
Awwlriiiight. I made up my mind.
I made it...
I was so happy. I stretched out on the sand and just laughed.
I went back to my friends. They were kickin' it drinking/smoking with reggae in the background...
I yelled, "YO!"
They said, "wuttuuup?"
"........."

鳥と会話

日本では、「いい体してる」とか、
「筋肉つけすぎだろ」って言われてた。

が、ハワイでは完全に小の小だった。
そのせいか、環境のせいか、人生で初めて本気で体を鍛えた。
週４で筋トレに行き、ジョギングはほぼ毎日してた。

海沿いの公園を何周も走って、
限界になったら靴とシャツを脱いで
静かな海に倒れこみ、
空を見ながらプカプカ浮かんで
体を冷やし、
公園のベンチに座って、
日向ぼっこで体を乾かした。

Conversation with the birds
In Japan, people told me I was well built, or sometimes too muscular.
But in Hawaii, I was definitely on the small side.
Maybe it was this embarrassment or the environment, but for the first time in my life, I started to seriously work out.
I went to the gym to lift 4 days a week, and jogged almost every day.
I did laps around the beach park until I was about to faint, then I'd take my shoes and shirt off, and collapse quietly into the water.
Cooled down my body while floating, looking up at the sky.
Then I sat on a bench and dried up in the sun.
There were always birds on the grass, resting. Most would fly away if you get close but one or two would remain and let me pet them.
These were incredible moments.
Divine, Spiritual moments.
Maybe that's why I'm being punished now…

芝には小鳥がいっぱい寝ていて、
近寄るとほとんどが逃げるけど、
必ず1、2羽は撫でさせてくれた。

**最高の時だった。
天国を味わってた
瞬間だった。**

だから罰があたったのかな……。

衝撃

僕が世の中で一番怖いものは、海とサメ。
2003年、13歳の女の子がサーフィン中、
4.5メートルのイタチザメに左腕を一口で噛みとられた。

体の血の60％をなくし、1か月近く入院、
だけど事件から1か月後にはなんとまたサーフィンしてた……。

それ以上に衝撃的だったのが、彼女へのインタビュー。
小さな13歳の女の子が、腕をサメに食いちぎられて言った言葉、

「他の人じゃなくて、私でよかった」

Shock
My biggest fear in life has always been the ocean and sharks.
In 2003, a 13-year-old girl had her left arm bit off in a single bite by a 4.5-meter tiger shark while surfing.
She lost 60% of her blood and was hospitalized for close to a month.
But a month after the incident, she was back on her surfboard…
What was even more shocking was her interview.
The words that came out of a little 13 year old girl, after her limb was bit off by a shark:
" I'm glad it was me and not anybody else."

サービス業

ハワイで就職した。
9・11後の最悪の経済状況のなか、
シェラトン・ワイキキという一流ホテルに、
友達のコネを使って入れた。

最初の部署はゲスト・サービス（ジム管理とコンシェルジュ）。
100ドルのチップを置いていく人もいれば、
いきなり怒鳴り始める日本のオヤジもいた。

そういうピンチで凹んでると上司が来て、
いまだに大事にしているアドバイスをくれた。

「サービス業に間違いは付き物。
それをどうフォローするかが勝負」

サービス業に限らない。

生きるってそういうことだと思う。

Service industry
My first real job was in Hawaii.
After 9.11, in the midst of the worst economy, my friend's dad "Franky," rest in peace, got me a job at one of the finest hotels, the Sheraton Waikiki.
I was first assigned to guest services (gym management and concierge). There were guests who would leave $100 tips. Then there were those grumpy old Japanese men who would start yelling at you out of the blue.
When I was feeling down and pretty much pissed off, my boss came and gave me a piece of advice which I still keep to heart.
"Mistakes are part of the service industry.
 What's important is how you follow up on it."
This is true not just about the service industry, **but about life.**

17時31分

シェラトンではコンベンション・サービス（イベント）も
やることになった。そこの環境が素晴らしかった。

タバコ部屋は2階の外。
ダイヤモンドヘッドを背景にワイキキビーチを眺めながら一服。

オフィス内には毎日、シェフ、搬入搬出、
音声などの人が行き来していて、笑い声が絶えなかった。
そして、17時31分になると必ず上司が来て、
「帰りなさい」と。

「あと少しだから」と言うと、

「私の責任だから、私が終わらせる。あなたは帰りな」と。

今思うと、恵まれすぎた毎日が当たり前になってた。

17:31

At Sheraton, I was transferred to Convention Services (events).
It was an amazing job.
The smoking area was just outside on the second floor, overlooking Waikiki Beach, with Diamond Head in the background.
It was a busy office with chefs, coordinators, and audio guys coming and going all day.
Always a lot of chitchat and laughter, every day.
And at 17:31, my boss would always come and tell me to go home.
When I would say, "I'll be done in just a bit" she always told me,
"This is my responsibility so I'll finish up. You go home."
Looking back, what was too good to be true had become the norm.

怖い男

ある日、仕事に向かうためバス停まで歩く途中。
200kg以上、2m以上、刺青だらけの、
超イカツイ男が前を歩いてた。

どっかの警備会社の制服を着て、
ちっちゃーいリュックをしょってた。

すると突然、立ち止まった。

でっかい腕を出し、木の枝を引っ張って、
咲いていた花を香った。
そして、また上機嫌に歩き出した。

信じられないほど
カッコ良かった……。

Scary guy
One day, I was on my way to the bus stop to go to work.
A giant, over 2m-tall and weighing over 200kg, fully tattooed was walking in front of me.
He was wearing a uniform of some security company with his tiny little backpack.
He suddenly stopped...
He stretched out his thick arm, grabs and pulls a branch close to smell the flower.
Then, the jolly ol'giant started walking again.
That was pretty cool...

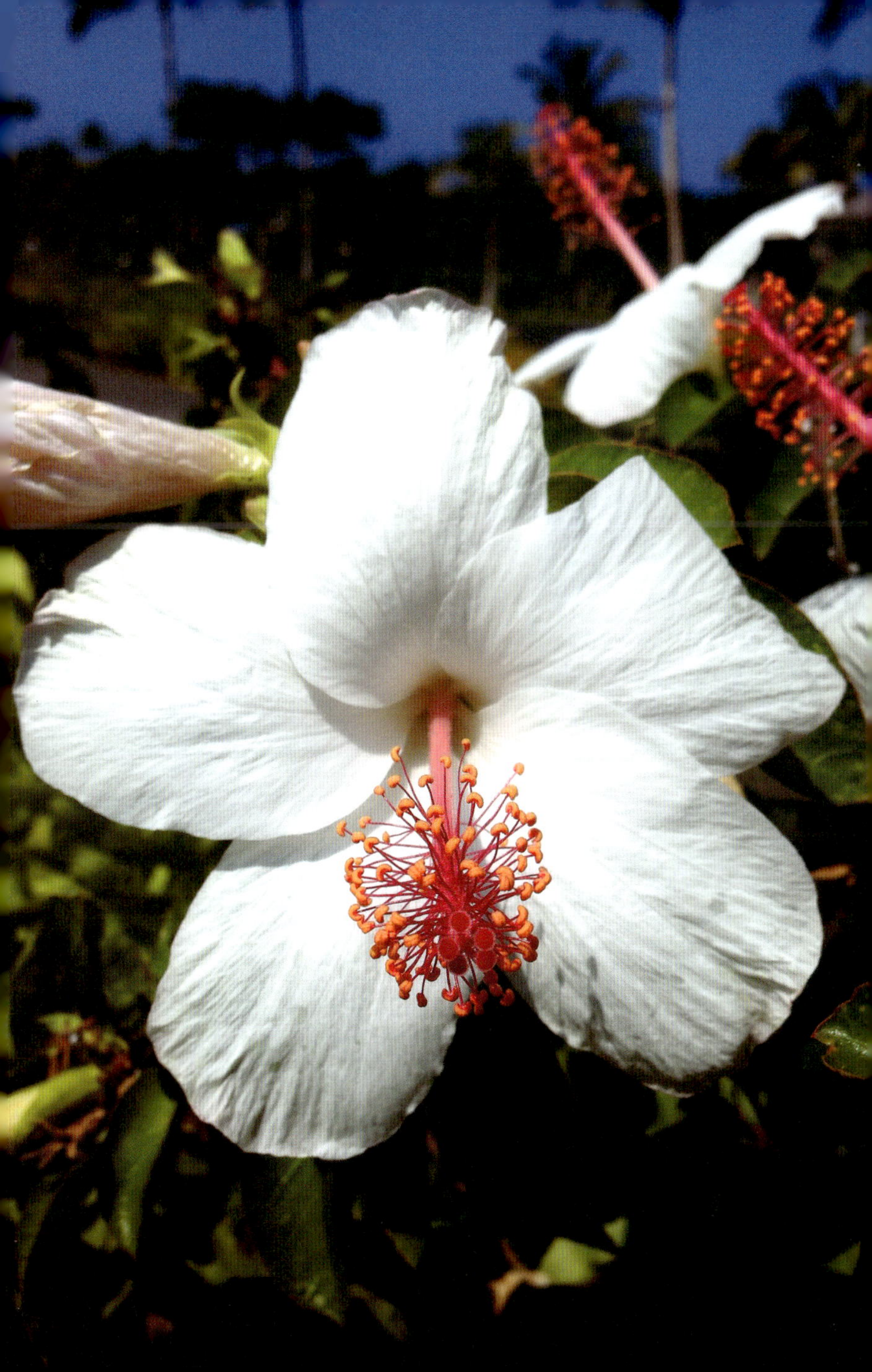

男気

ある夜、クラブを出ると、
ハワイ人対サモア人で20人ぐらいのケンカをしていた。

しかも全員、まるでマーク・ハントやジェロム・レ・バンナみたい。
重量級なのに速い！

もう気絶している男の頭を蹴り飛ばしてたり……と、
見とれてる間に囲まれた。

後ろには誰かの車、前方左右では殺し合い。

「ヤバイ！　巻き添えをくらう！」

と思ったそのとき、隣に自分の半分ぐらいの小さな女の子がいた。

彼女に腕を回した。
彼女を守るため……ではなく、守ってもらうためだ。

ハワイの大男で、小さい女の子に手を出すバカは少ない。
それを知ってるその子も、僕を見て、

「つかまってな」

と。
恥ずかしながら、男らしく、そうさせていただいて
助かった……（笑）。

My manly stance...

One night, when I stepped out of a club, there were about 20 Hawaiians and Samoans in a fight.
And they were all like Mark Hunt or Jerome Le Banner, heavyweights but fast.
Stomping in the heads of already-unconscious men, the whole deal...
I was excited watching, and before I knew it, I was surrounded.
Someone's car was behind me and heads getting knocked off all around.
"Ohhh snap. It's going to be my head soon enough!"
Then I noticed a small girl next to me, half my size, stuck too.
I put my arms around her to protect her.
I wish, but not really...
For her to protect ME!
Not many giants are cruel enough to lay a hand on a small girl.
She knew this too so she looked at me and said,
"Yeap, you better hold on."
And yes I did, in my manly stance...

CHAPTER 4
24〜30 years old

Tokyo
東京

マッキャンエリクソン就職

大学2年生のころから、外資系広告会社マッキャンエリクソンの
戦略プランニング部が第一志望だった。

なぜって、グローバル的には広告といえば、マッキャンだったから。

が、勉強するほうでもなく、9・11のテロがあったりで、
ハワイで1年ホテルマンをやって、
ビザの期限を理由にいきなり帰国。
その後、歌舞伎町でプラカード持ちをしたり、
空いた時間には外資系広告会社Sでインターン、
タダ働きをしたりしていた。

その間、毎週2回、マッキャンの戦略プランニング部トップの
オーストラリア人に電話を入れることを習慣にした。
それが半年間続いた。

何回か話せたけど、大半の場合は居留守を使われているのか、
アシスタントの方とのやりとりだった。

嫌がられても覚えてもらうのが必要と思い、続けた。
すると、結局、遊びで得たコネを3つ見つけた。

McCANN

Job at McCann Erickson Japan

Since my sophomore year in university I've wanted to work in the strategic planning division at the international advertising agency, McCann Erickson. Why? From a global perspective, advertising meant McCann to me.

9.11 happened and after a year of working in the hotel business, I had to go back to Japan due to visa issues.

Once back, I held signboards in the city of Kabukicho and on my days off worked as an intern for free at another ad agency.

Meanwhile, I made it a routine to call the Aussie director of McCann Japan's strategic planning division on the phone at least twice a week.

This lasted for six months.

I was able to talk to him a couple of times but mostly he was 'unavailable' so I left messages with his assistant.

Even if he thought it was annoying, I figured it's more important to leave an impression so I kept at it.

Eventually, I stumbled upon 3 connections through my past.

イギリス時代の近所の友達:「一切採用してない」
その友達の知り合い:「すみません、まだポジションがなく〜」
そしてハワイの仲間の父親:「来週空いていますか？」

すぐ、面談が決まった。

面接室に入ったら、「おまえは皆知ってるなー」と言われた。
僕はニヤッとして、

「で？」

と言った。
そして2004年３月、晴れて就職が決まった。

勝ちー！

A friend from the neighborhood in the U.K.: "Sorry no chance, no position."
A friend of that friend: "Sorry, we're trying but don't have a position yet..."
And the father of my buddy from Hawaii: "Are you available next week?"
I got an interview.
As soon as I entered the room, his first comment was,
"You know everybody huh?!"
I smiled and said,
"So?"
In March 2004, I got the job!
I win.

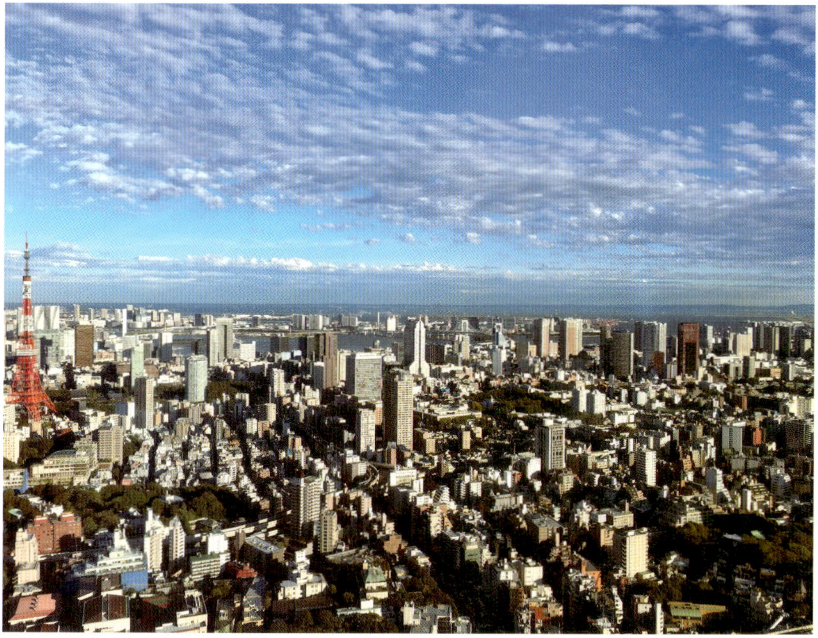

いきなりクビ？

会社に入って2週間目、週末に友達のライブとインタビューを、
ビデオに撮ることになった。

金曜日、会社のビデオカメラを持って友達のライブに繰り出した。
その日のことはあまり覚えていない。
インタビューはした……。
けどそれ以上にいっぱい飲んで、騒いだ。

翌朝目が覚めて、すぐに体中から冷や汗が出た。
カ、カメラがない……。
電車の棚に置いたように思うけど思い出せない。
急いで鉄道会社に電話したけど、届け出はないとのことだった。
終わったかな、と思った。

入ってひと月も経たないうちに会社のビデオをなくすような奴は
クビにされても仕方ない。

翌週、死にたい気持ちで出社し、
上司に「実は……」と打ち明けた。

一瞬硬い表情になった上司ではあったが、
一言「しょうがないじゃん。ないんでしょ」と。

どうやらクビは免れた。
だけどあっさり許された分、だらしない自分が悔しかった。
頭を下げて上司に謝りながら感謝した。

Fired already?
Two weeks into the job, I had an assignment to film my friend's gig and interview him.
On Friday, I took the company video camera and went to the show.
Honestly, I don't remember much of what happened that day.
I know I did the interview...
But I also know I drank and partied hard that night.
The next morning, I woke up and literally froze.
"Where's the video camera…?"
Maybe I left it on the shelf on the train...
I called the rail company but no luck...
I thought I was finished.
A guy who loses the company video camera not even a month into the job is bound to get fired.
Monday.
I got to the office... felt like killing myself.
Told my boss.
For a while, he had a stern look.
But then he said,
"Well, what's lost is lost right?"
I still had a job...
But because I was let off so easy,
it frustrated me so much for being such a hack. Never again.
I bowed sincerely before my boss to express my deepest apology and gratitude.

おとなのおもちゃ？

ある日、机で仕事をしていると、突然、
副社長のオフィスにもう一人のプランナーと一緒に呼ばれた。

ボスの前に座ると、
カタログのようなものを手渡された。

「昨日、ドイツから客が来て、
このカタログを置いていったんだけど、どう思う？」

カタログを開けてみると、
ありとあらゆる「大人のおもちゃ」の写真が並んでいる。
どう思う？って……。

製品の色？　形？　サイズ？
カタログのレイアウト？　マーケティング戦略？
それとも、個人的に使ったことがあるかってこと？

Adult toys?!
One day, I was called in to the VP's office with another planner.
We sat down in front of the boss and were handed what looked like a catalogue.
"Yesterday, I had a visitor from Germany and he left this catalogue. What do you think?"
I opened the catalogue and there were pictures of sex toys.
What do you mean, what do I think...?!
Do you mean about the color? The shape? The size?
Or does he want to hear what I think about the layout of the catalogue?
Or the marketing strategy?
Whether I've used them myself before???

返答に困っていると、ボスが、

「ま、この仕事をしていると、
たまにはこんな楽しいカタログも見られるってことなんだよね（笑）」

その後、大人のおもちゃとは関係のない世間話をしばらくして、
ミーティング終了。

一緒に呼ばれたプランナーと二人で、
ミーティングの真意は一体なんだったのか、
タバコをふかしながら考えた。

とにかく、あんなカタログが普通においてあるオフィスは
ヘンだけど面白いし、それを見せてくれつつ、
この仕事の楽しさを教えようとしてくれたボスも
ヘンだけど、なんか、良い。

広告会社のプランナーって、ホントに良い仕事だ。

As we sat there trying to figure out what to say, he says
"When you're in this business, sometimes you get to see fun catalogues like this(laugh)."
After that, we just talked about the weekend and the meeting was over.
The two of us left the room and went outside to have a smoke, thinking about what the actual intent of the meeting was.
Whatever it was, it's weird and fun that such a catalogue is laying around in the workplace and what's more strange but great is that the boss shows it to us to try and tell us about the good aspect of this job.
Being a planner at an ad agency is pretty awesome.

愛のムチ

先輩方に叱られまくって、育った。

「そんな態度で仕事してるんだったら、
サラリーマン失格。やめちまえ！」

「なんだその電話の出方は？
そんぐらい日本の常識だぞ！」

「おまえのなかで話をまとめてから俺には話せ！」

「おまえの意見なんて聞いてねーよ！　今はただやれ！」

「さっきから、おまえの"オッケ"って返事、ナメてんの？」

「アツイのはいいけど、
いつか周りがついて行けなくならないようにな」

「殺すぞ！　いや、殺すのも面倒くせえ、死んでこい！」

毎日、「おい、アホ、今日はこれとこれと（15個ぐらい）やれ」
（これは同僚だったアメリカ人ショーンの言葉。
彼は若くして亡くなってしまった。
今の僕を誇りに思ってくれているとうれしいです。
一緒にまたビールを飲むのが楽しみです。
まだちょっと待っててください）

先輩方は本気で叱ってくれた。
いちいち目が覚めた。
その後、彼らとは皆、特に仲良くしてもらった。
今、そのときの先輩の言葉、気持ちには感謝しかない。

Tough Love
I became a better planner thanks to the constant scolding from my seniors.
"If that's your attitude, you have no right to be a businessman. Just quit already!"
"THAT'S how you answer the phone?! This is common sense in Japan!"
 (Phone mannerism is really important in Japan)
"Don't talk to me before you organize what you're gonna say!"
"No one's asking for your opinion! You just do it!"
"When you respond to me with that "OK" shit, are you trying to piss me off?"
"It's all good to be passionate but make sure you don't lose the others along the way."
"I'll kill you! Actually, I can't even be bothered to, just go kill yourself!"
Every day, it was, "Hey stupid, do this and this and this (about 15 in total) by the end of the day."
(This last one were the words of my American colleague, Sean. He passed away at a young age. I only hope he's proud of me now. Looking forward to having a pint with you soon sir. But not yet)
My seniors scolded at me seriously.
And it opened my eyes each time.
After that, I became particularly close to all of them.
Now, the only thing I can say is thank you, for their words, their passion, and their devotion...to kicking my ass when needed.

TGIF

金曜日の夕方になると、周りの同僚たちに、

「今日は祝・金曜日ですよ〜」

と伝えてまわるのが、先輩から受け継いだ僕の役目だった。

この業界、金曜日の夜はおろか、
土日も仕事をする人が
フツーにいる。

ちゃんと遊べない人は、
ちゃんと仕事もできない。

逆も言える。
フライデーナイトぐらい楽しもうよ。
そうだ、六本木へ行こう。

TGIF
On Fridays, it was my duty to remind people to Thank God It's Friday!
A ritual passed down to me from my first mentor & friend from McCann.
In this industry, in Japan, people work through Friday nights as well as the weekend, treating it like any other work day.
If you don't know how to play well, you can't work well. Vice versa.
It's Friday night, so let's enjoy.
That's right, let's get crunk, drunk, wild, ape shit, whatever.
Just please get the hell out of the office.

＊ TGIF …… 「Thank God, It's Friday」の頭文字。

手ブラ（手に何も持たないほうね）をすすめる

会社にいくときは、カバンを持たない派。
通勤は人間観察の時間、街を見ながら企画を妄想する時間、
ニュースを見る時間だから、
携帯、財布、カギ、タバコさえあれば事が足りる。

だから、あえてあれこれと荷物を持たない。
それと……、
遅刻しても、会社抜け出しても、
目立たない。

Always empty-handed
I never carried a bag to the office.
The commute is time for observing people, to brainstorm plans as I walk through the city, to read/watch the news.
So all I need is my phone, wallet, keys, and cigs.
So I choose not to carry...whatever is in that bag of yours.
More importantly, you don't stand out if you're late or if you want to sneak home early...

インフルエンサー・マーケティング

僕は広告が嫌いだ。だからこそ魅力を感じた。
基本は邪魔な物を使って、人の行動に影響を与える。

広告がなかなか効かないと言われるずっと前から
影響力のある国内外の名だたるクリエイターたちとコラボして
あれこれ仕掛けてきた。

インフルエンサー・マーケティングというが、
それが普通の人と人のコミュニケーションだと思う。

白髪を染め、年齢を隠して「僕も若者！　僕、友達！」
って口説くのではなく、
白髪を出してオヤジらしく、渋く、その若者文化の創作に手を貸す。
そして、若者自身には「その文化に自分が貢献している」気持ちから
生まれるオーナーシップを持たせる。
その経験自体にブランドの世界観を語らせればよい。
うそ臭くない。

Influencer marketing
I hate advertising. That's why this job was so appealing.
Change human behavior positively with something that is generally considered disturbing, annoying, or a waste of time.
Long before ads were said to have less impact,
I have worked with influential creators, domestic and abroad, to run various initiatives.
Many call this influencer marketing but it's simple communication between people.
It's not about dying your hair to hide your age and try to be included as a part of young culture, but about showing your experienced greys; Lending a hand to the young to feel as they're contributing to the creation of that culture. Give them ownership and let that experience do the talking about your brand.

やめて

仕事の一番キライな点は、
ネガティブ・チェックだらけの長い打ち合わせ。

「なぜできないか」だけでは素人目線だ。
「どうすればできるか」を探すのが仕事。

代案や解決策があるならまだしも、
何も考えずに気安く「できない」発言する奴は
外に出ていてほしい。

ALSに関しても「できない」理由ばかり言わないで、
うそでも、妄想でもいいから、

「できる」「治る」「元の生活に戻れる」理由を教えてくれ。

Stop it

The worst part of this job is the long meetings filled with "negative checks."
Identifying why you cannot do something is for amateurs.
Being a professional is about identifying how to make it possible.
If you have alternatives and solutions then you can shoot down others' ideas.
But those who don't give that much thought and easily say, "Can't do it" have no place in meetings.
With ALS, too.
PLEASE don't tell me reasons why it can't be done anymore.
Lie to me!
Tell me we're close to a cure.
Tell me how it's going to work.
Tell me I'm going to get my life back...even if it's just a fairy tale.

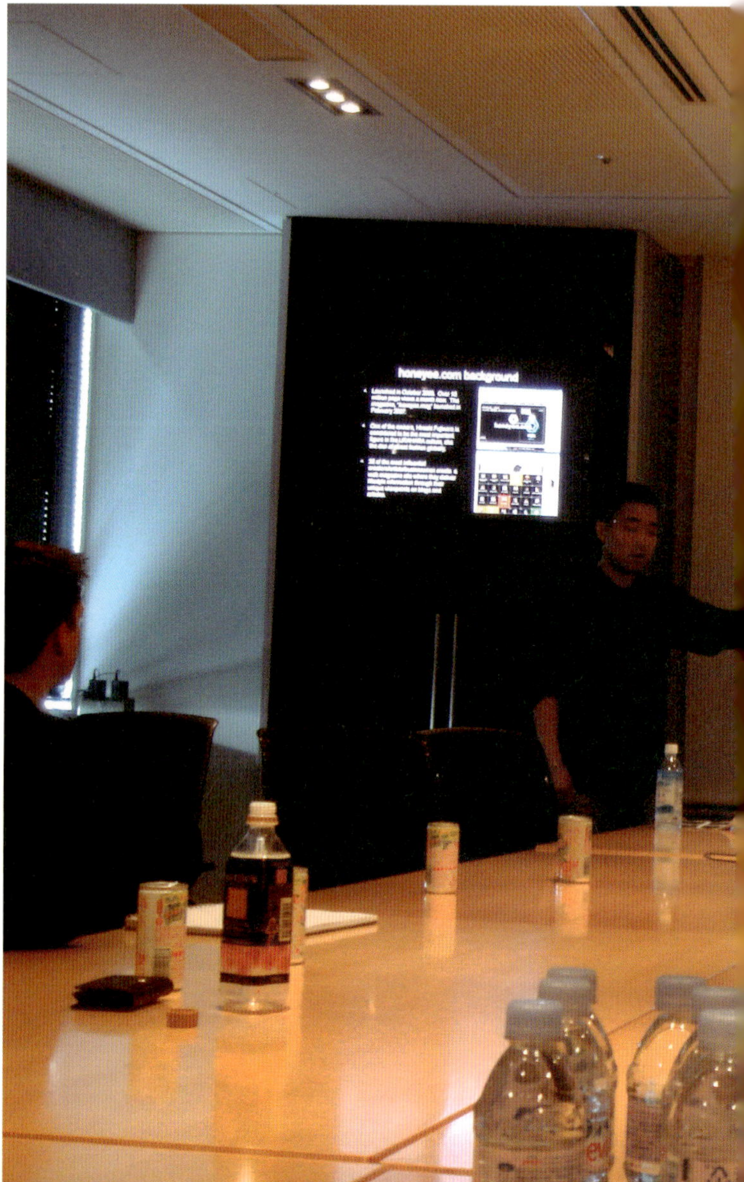
honeyee.com background

honeyee.com background

aunched in October 2005. Over 10
illion page views a month now. The
agazine, "honeyee.mag" launched in
ebruary 2007.

ne of the owners, Hiroshi Fujiwara is
nsidered to be the most important
ure in the URAHARA culture, aka
e don of street fashion globally.

f the most influential
ors/artists/businessmen create a
b magazine site where they deliver
yle information through their
que viewpoints on blogs and
cles

ピッチ

企業が広告を任せる会社を決めるための競合。
大好きだ。メチャ張り切った。試合。勝負。

日本を代表する他社にも、外資のライバルにも
どうしても負ける気がしなかった。
そして実際、勝つと快感すぎた。

今まで自分を受け入れてくれなかった日本に
勝った気が勝手にしてた。

大きいピッチになると
海外からグローバルチームの豪腕が送られてきた。
自分は大抵、グローバルチーム、日本のマネージメント、
日本の現場のチームの間に置かれていた。

大変だったけど楽しかった。
一番成長した時期だった。

宝物です。

The pitch

A competition between agencies where the client decides who to assign their marketing communication to. I love it. The adrenalin. It's game time. I never feel like we can lose, whether it's versus a top domestic agency or our international competitors. When you win, the rush is incredible. Personally, especially against the dominant domestic agencies, every victory felt like getting back a piece of me from Japan, "the society who refused to accept me until, now." When it's a big pitch, we would normally get the big guns from the global teams to help us out. This usually meant I was put between the global team, the Japan team, and senior management. It was hectic but a lot of fun.
It was when I learned the most. **A priceless experience I treasure.**

目的

一番よく見失われるもの。

どんなに小さいことを話していても、考えていても、
常に感じていなければいけない。

よくあるのが、最終的な目的を見失った議論。

「ん～、で？」

って言いたくなる。

結果がすべての国際的な場では相手にされない。
仕事だけじゃなく、プライベートでもそう。

目的を見失われたALSについての議論、
どれぐらい行われているんだろう……。

Objective
What's lost so often.
No matter how small the topic is, it always has to be top of mind as you talk.
Too often there are discussions where the ultimate goal is lost.
Makes you ask, "so?" or "and?"
It's even more important in an international scene where results are everything. It goes for both work and private life.
It makes me wonder how many discussions on ALS out there are "lost"...

部内に送ったメール

From: Fujita, (HIRO) Masahiro (TYO-MEW)
Sent: Monday, November 15, 2010 5:01 PM
To: TYO ME Planning Users
Subject: 藤田正裕、負傷
Importance: Low

お疲れ様です。

個人ごとで申し訳ないのですが、
明日から１週間〜10日ぐらい検査で入院することになりました。
決してズル休みではありません。
決して家でコールオブデューティーで遊ぶわけではありません。
実は７月ぐらいから左腕に力が入らず、
今は左足も同じで少しずつ右側にも症状が見えてきました。
で医者にずっと検査してもらっているのですが
原因がわからないとのことで検査入院となりました。
また言っておきますが、
決してマカオに旅に出るわけではありません。
決して一足先にスノボではありません。

この間、メールはあまり見れないと思います。
いない間いろいろとご迷惑お掛けしますが、宜しくお願いします。
来週の半ばには戻れると思います。

皆様もお体には気をつけてください。

ヒロ

Email to the department

From: Fujita, (HIRO) Masahiro (TYO-MEW)
Sent: Monday, November 15, 2010 5:01 PM
To: TYO ME Planning Users
Subject: Masahiro Fujita, injured
Importance: Low

Unfortunately, I will be in the hospital from tomorrow, for a week to 10 days for tests.
No, I am not lying.
No, this is not an excuse to play Call of Duty at home.
In fact, from July, I haven't been able to lift my left arm as I used to and now I'm starting to get similar symptoms in my left leg and slightly on my right side as well.
Doctors have been running tests but they can't find the cause, so I was told that I need to be hospitalized for more tests.
Again.
No, I am not going on a holiday to Macau.
No, I am not planning an early snowboarding trip.
I won't have much access to the internet.
Apologies for the trouble while I am away.
I hope to be back in the office by middle of next week.

Thank you,
Hiro

CHAPTER 5
30〜XX years old

ALS
筋萎縮性側索硬化症

検査入院

腕や足が上がりにくく、体が弱くなって数か月、
検査入院することになった。
1週間検査をやって、薬をもらって終わりかなと思っていた。

一人で入院手続きなどをし、
「ちょっとした休暇だ」としか思っていなかった。
途中で友達に迎えに来てもらい、池袋で飲んだりもした。
すると毎日検査が続き、なぜか2週目に突入。

脊髄から水を取ったり、筋電図という検査も2回行われた。
筋電図とは、針を2〜3センチほど筋肉に刺し、
電波が筋肉を通っているかを調べるもの。
スネ、もも、手、腕、肩、首筋など、
体中に針を刺して力を入れるという、拷問のような検査だ。

そのときぐらいから
「どんだけやばいんだよ」 と思い始めた……。

The Hospital for tests
After a few months, it became really difficult to lift my arms and legs so I was admitted to the hospital for some tests.
I figured they would run tests for a week, give me some meds and that would be the end of it.
I checked myself into the hospital thinking, "this'll be a short break."
I even had a friend come and pick me up and we went for a drink in Ikebukuro.
But the tests continued into a second week…
They took samples of my spinal cord fluid and ran electromyograms, twice.
This is a test where they stick a needle 2-3cm into your muscle to measure if it's functioning right.
It's pretty much torture. They stick a thick needle all over the body one place at a time and ask to flex your muscle. My shins, thighs, hands, arms, shoulders, neck, back…
It was around that time when I started thinking to myself, **" How fucked up am I…"**

宣告

先生たちから「親も呼んだほうが」と言われた。
「なんだよ大げさだな」と思い、兄と二人で話を聞くことにした。

病棟の小さな会議室に、先生二人、兄弟二人。
2010年11月26日、ALSと宣告された。
先生がこの病気のことを細かく説明してくれたが、
内容はほとんど覚えていない。ただ、

「ゆっくり全身麻痺になり、死ぬ。そして治療薬はない」

ということだけわかった。

The Diagnosis
The doctors said that I should have my parents present.
I thought they were just over-reacting so I just had my brother there.
It was in a small meeting room in the hospital..
Just two doctors, my brother and I.
On November 26th of 2010 I was told that I have ALS.
The doctors went into detail about the disease.
I hardly heard a word they said…
All I heard was,
"Your body will slowly become paralyzed and you will die. There is no cure."

心境は説明できない。

その瞬間から、人生が変わるのを体全体で感じた。

兄と目を合わせて「ウソだろ」と
心の中でボソッとつぶやいた。

I can't explain what that felt like.
But my whole body understood that EVERYTHING about my life was about to change.
My brother and I looked at each other and I silently said,
"You're kidding right…"

その後、二人で病院の周りを歩いた。
泣いて、笑って、怒って、狂った……。
近くのお寺で手を合わせた。
「助けてください」から「テメーも死ね」まで、
わけがわからなかった。

その夜、一人でひたすらYouTubeでALSのビデオを見た。
つらいどころじゃなかったけど、
「逃げちゃいけない」と、調べまくった。

変な冷静さから、突然、
心拍数500ぐらいの気持ちを繰り返し、
一睡もできなかった。

Afterwards, my brother and I walked around the hospital.
We cried, laughed, got angry, and went crazy...
We went to a shrine close by and prayed. I said everything from
"Please help me" to "I'm gonna kill YOU"
I was going insane...
That night, I watched every video about ALS on You Tube.
It was hard but I knew I couldn't run away.
I wanted to learn everything I could about my new friend.
I would be strangely calm and then suddenly my heartbeat would jump to 500bps.
I was up all night on this rollercoaster of emotions.

引っ越し

当時、エレベーターがないマンションの4階に住んでいた。
退院後、階段がもう上れないので、
エレベーター付きの広めの物件を急いで兄と探した。
富士山も見える完璧な物件を探せた。

もちろん、「実家に戻れば？」と何万回も言われた。
兄は「世界中の、行きたい・見たいところに全部行けばいい。
カネのことは心配するな」と言ってくれた。
けど、今までの生活を取り上げられそうになると、
余計に普通の生活がしたくなる。

「死ぬための思い出作りや準備をするつもりはない」

としか言えなかった。
たしか、治ったらトライアスロンを完走するとも言ってたと思う。
なにを言ってんのか……昔から、とにかく負けを認めるのは
得意じゃなかった。
で、会社に復帰。一人暮らしに戻り、「闘病との生活」が始まった。

The Move

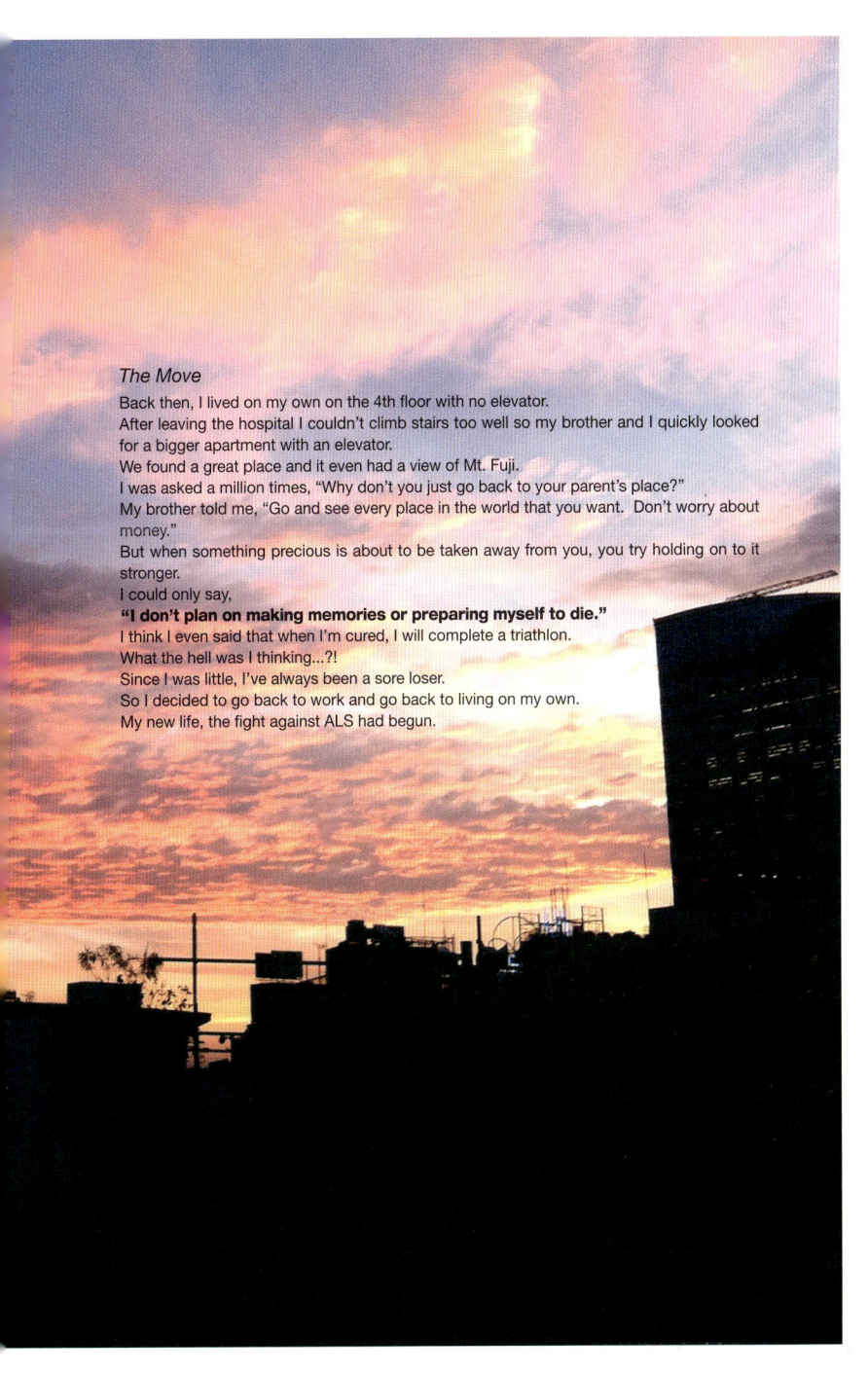

Back then, I lived on my own on the 4th floor with no elevator.
After leaving the hospital I couldn't climb stairs too well so my brother and I quickly looked for a bigger apartment with an elevator.
We found a great place and it even had a view of Mt. Fuji.
I was asked a million times, "Why don't you just go back to your parent's place?"
My brother told me, "Go and see every place in the world that you want. Don't worry about money."
But when something precious is about to be taken away from you, you try holding on to it stronger.
I could only say,
"I don't plan on making memories or preparing myself to die."
I think I even said that when I'm cured, I will complete a triathlon.
What the hell was I thinking...?!
Since I was little, I've always been a sore loser.
So I decided to go back to work and go back to living on my own.
My new life, the fight against ALS had begun.

松岡修造

ALSと診断されて間もなく、狂っていたころ、
テレビで、松岡修造さんが子どもにテニスを指導する、
修造チャレンジの番組をやっていた。

松岡さんのファンというわけでもなかったが、
次の瞬間、また人生が変わった。

弱気になって泣いている小学生に向かって、松岡さんは
目を充血させながら、ラケットを地面に叩きつけ、大声で、

「できるって言え!」

と言い放った。

聞きたかった言葉を、
聞きたかった口調で言われ、胸をえぐられた。
それが僕を戦闘モードにしてくれたと言っても過言ではない。

小学生にも、なんでも本気で立ち向かう松岡さん、
ホントにありがとうございます。

生きる力になっています。

Shuzo Matsuoka
In the early days after the diagnosis when I was still going crazy,
I saw a program called the Shuzo Challenge on TV.
It was about the former professional tennis player, Shuzo Matsuoka, teaching kids how to play tennis.
I wasn't necessarily a fan or anything but in the next moment, my life changed, yet again.
An elementary school kid had lost his confidence and was crying.
Matsuoka-san ran up to him slamming his racket on the ground, with blood-shot eyes, and yelled,
"SAY THAT YOU CAN DO IT! SAY IT!!"

The exact words in the exact tone that I needed to hear.
It's not an over-statement to say those words are what put me into my fight mode.
Matsuoka-san, who gives 100% to everything.
Thank you.
You helped me find the courage to live.

反応

この病気のことをみんなに伝えるために、何百回説明しただろう。
一人一人、反応がぜんぜん違う。
こんな状況なのに、すごい人間観察の経験をしていた。
言葉を失ったり、笑いに変えようとしたり、
泣いたり、強がったり……。

不思議なのが、どんな反応に対しても、
自分は気分を害することがなかった。

**繰り返し説明することが、
心のリハビリになっていたのかも
しれない。**

Reactions
I can't recall how many times I explained the disease to people.
Everybody had a different reaction.
Some lose their words.
Some try to laugh about it,
Some cry about it, or act tough.
Surprisingly, whatever their reaction,
I didn't feel offended at all.
This constant repetition of the explanation probably worked as rehab for my soul.

3・11

20階のオフィスで、最初はゆっくりだった揺れが、
これまでにない大きな地震になっていった。

机の上の書類はふっとび、椅子も左右に大きく動いた。
机の下にもぐる皆。

僕は床に手をついちゃうと立ち上がれない状態だったので
椅子に座ったまま、机を必死に掴んでいた。

「キャー」が「ギャー!」に、やがて「シーン」となった。
(人はホントに怖いとき、声は出ない)

2度目の大きな揺れがおさまり、みんなで下に逃げることになった。
ただでさえ、この時期には50歩ぐらいしか歩けなかった。
エレベーターはもちろん動いていない。どうしよう……。

僕の脚が思うように動かないことを知っている先輩や後輩たちが、
壁が崩れるなか、肩を貸してくれたり、
かついでくれたりして20階分の階段を下りた。

3.11

Initially, the shaking was rather slow on the 20th floor of the office. But it soon became the biggest ever. The papers and files flew off our desks. Chairs rolled from one side of the office to the other. Everyone took cover underneath their desks. By this time my ALS had progressed to a point where I couldn't get up once I put my hands on the floor. So I stayed in my seat and held my desk as tight as I could. The screaming gradually got louder and eventually turned into complete silence. (When people are truly scared, they can't scream) After the second big shake everybody started to escape to the ground floor. I could barely walk 50 steps at that stage... The elevators weren't running... I didn't know what to do... My seniors and colleagues who knew that my legs weren't as mobile, lent me their shoulders, and sometimes even carried me on their backs as the walls crumbled around us. They helped me down the 20 floors of stairs.

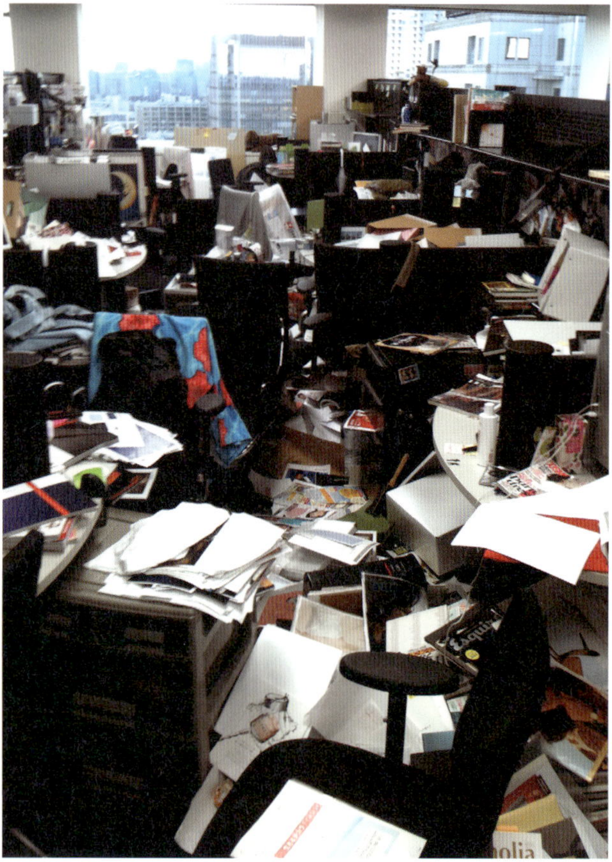

本当にありがたかった。
と同時に、鳥肌が立つほど
恐ろしかった。

なぜなら、今、自分のせいで何人もの命を犠牲にするかもしれない。
その日から、出社は週一になった。

道路はすでに車がぎっしりと詰まって、
家に向かう人たちが大勢歩き出していた。
携帯電話はまったくつながらない。

寒いなか、会社の仲間たちは、僕のために通りに出て、
タクシーを拾ってくれようとしていた。
でも、タクシーはぜんぜん来ない。

しかたなく、ビルの喫茶店に戻り、何人かで待機することにした。
僕はそのうち友達と連絡がついて、車で迎えに来てもらえると
思っていたので、「僕にかまわず帰ってください」と伝えた。
でも、電車が止まって帰れない人もいて、
多くの仲間が喫茶店にとどまった。

誰かのワンセグテレビから、お台場が燃えているとか、
東北がひどいといった情報が流れてきた。
その間も、小さな揺れが続き、そのたびに不安は増す一方だった。
けど、自分ではなにもできない……。

すると、後輩の一人が、

「ビルの病院に行けば車椅子があるはず。借りてきます！」

と言って店を飛び出した。そして、しばらく経って、
車椅子を手に戻ってきた。

「病院にはなかったんですが、ビルの管理事務所にあると
教えてもらって、借りてきました！　僕の家はここから歩けます。
ヒロさん、一緒に帰りましょう」

**ブレイクスルーとはこのことだ。
仕事ができる人は、こういう状況でも頼りになる。**
ゆっくりと車椅子を押してもらい、後輩の家に向かった。

30分くらいかかって後輩のアパートにたどり着き、
ほっと一息つくことができた。

夜になると電話もつながるようになり、
家族や友人とも連絡がとれた。でも、道路は車が動く状態ではなく、
一晩、後輩の家に泊まらせてもらうことにした。

翌日、その後輩が東京に残っていた最後の一台だったという
レンタカーを手に入れ、初台の僕の家まで連れていってくれた。
彼は、奥さんが仙台に行っていた先輩に車を貸すと言って
すぐに出て行った。
**やっぱり仕事ができる人は、
こういう状況でも頼りになる。**

しばらく余震は続き、福島原発も恐ろしいことになっていた。
でも僕はどこへも動けず、自分の部屋にいるしかなかった。
そして、友達が来た……。

世界が衝撃を受けた、3・11。
東北の人たちには申し訳なく、助けることはおろか、
助けてもらわないと生きられない自分がいた。
ALSの、これからの生活の、大変さを感じた。

そして、この時期から、車椅子での生活が急激に増えた。
正直、見られるのが恥ずかしかったが、日本の復興と同時に、
僕の意地やプライドを少しずつ
削る作業が始まっていた。

P111 **Of course, I was thankful from the bottom of my heart.**
But I was also, absolutely terrified.
My existence had risked the lives of so many people.
Fathers, sons, daughters, husbands...
From that day onward I decided to go into the office only once a week.
The roads were already packed with cars.
Crowds of people were walking, desperate to get home.
No calls were going through on our cell phones.
It was freezing but my colleagues were out on the street, trying to flag down a cab for me with no luck...all occupied.
So some of us went back inside a coffee shop in the building and decided to wait.
I figured I would eventually get through to one of my friends who will come and pick me up so I told them, "I'll be fine, please go home."
But some couldn't go home as there were no trains so a lot of us decided to wait it out.
From someone's one-seg TV, we started to get some information.
Fire was breaking out in Odaiba, and the Tohoku-the North Eastern area had serious damage.
All throughout, the aftershocks continued and each time, our fear grew greater.
But there wasn't anything I could do on my own...

P112 Soon, one of my colleagues jumped up and said "There may be a wheelchair at that hospital over there.
 I'll go and see if I can borrow one!"
He ran out of the coffee shop and a short while later returned with a wheelchair.
"They didn't have one at the hospital but they told me that the building office may have one and they did! I can walk home from here so Hiro-san, let's go home together!"
A breakthrough...
People who excel in their jobs are reliable, even at times like this.
He slowly pushed the wheelchair and I went to his home.
It took about 30 minutes to get to his apartment and we were finally able to sit back in relief.
It was already late evening when the phone calls finally got through and I was able to speak to my family and friends.
But traffic was crazy, so I decided to spend the night at his house.
The next day, my colleague again, miraculously got ahold of the only rental car left in Tokyo and drove me back to my home in Hatsudai.
Then went to go lend the car to another colleague, whose wife was in Sendai.
Again, people who excel in their jobs are reliable, even at times like this.

P113 The aftershock continued for a while and soon the horror of the Fukushima Nuclear Plant became evident.
I couldn't go anywhere so I just stayed in my room.
Then my friends came over...
3.11 shocked the world.
With much empathy for the people of Tohoku,
I found myself not being able to help at all.
Furthermore, I couldn't do a damn thing without help myself...
The difficulty of life with ALS, of my days ahead, started to show its true colors.
From this day, I spent more time in the wheelchair than before.
The process of throwing away my ego and pride was well underway...

僕のトビー

パソコンを打つことが難しくなり、視線とまばたきで操作できるトビー社のアイトラッキングシステム を使い始めた。
一言、素晴らしい。

インターネットからパワーポイントまで、かなり楽にできる。
「年配の方には難しい」と言う人もいるが、それは違う。

わが子と話すためだったら、お安い御用だと思う。
年配の気力をなめちゃダメ。

My Tobii

I started using the Tobii eye tracking system and it's pretty much awesome.
From surfing the Internet to making PowerPoint.
Easy…
Some say it would be hard for elders to use, but they're wrong.
If that's what it takes to speak to your child it will get done.
You can't underestimate the will power of elders.

最強の無言

ある夜、中学時代の仲間たちと集まって飲んでた。
一人に付き合ってくれと言って、外まで車椅子を押してもらった。
みんなといたせいで気が高ぶっていたのかもしれない。
外で大泣きした。
するとそいつは少しも動かず、一言も話さず、
10分ぐらい、ただ立って同じ方向を見ていた。

そのとき
一番必要としていた、
最高のなぐさめだった……。

The most powerful silence
One night, I got together with my junior high school friends for drinks.
I asked one of them to help me out of the house on the wheelchair for some fresh air...
It was probably the alcohol and the high of being with the fam.
I suddenly started to cry my heart out outside.
My buddy didn't move an inch, and didn't say a word.
Just stood by me for about ten minutes, staring into the distance, in the same direction.
**It was one of the deepest and most heartfelt "words" of support
that I needed to "hear" at that time...**

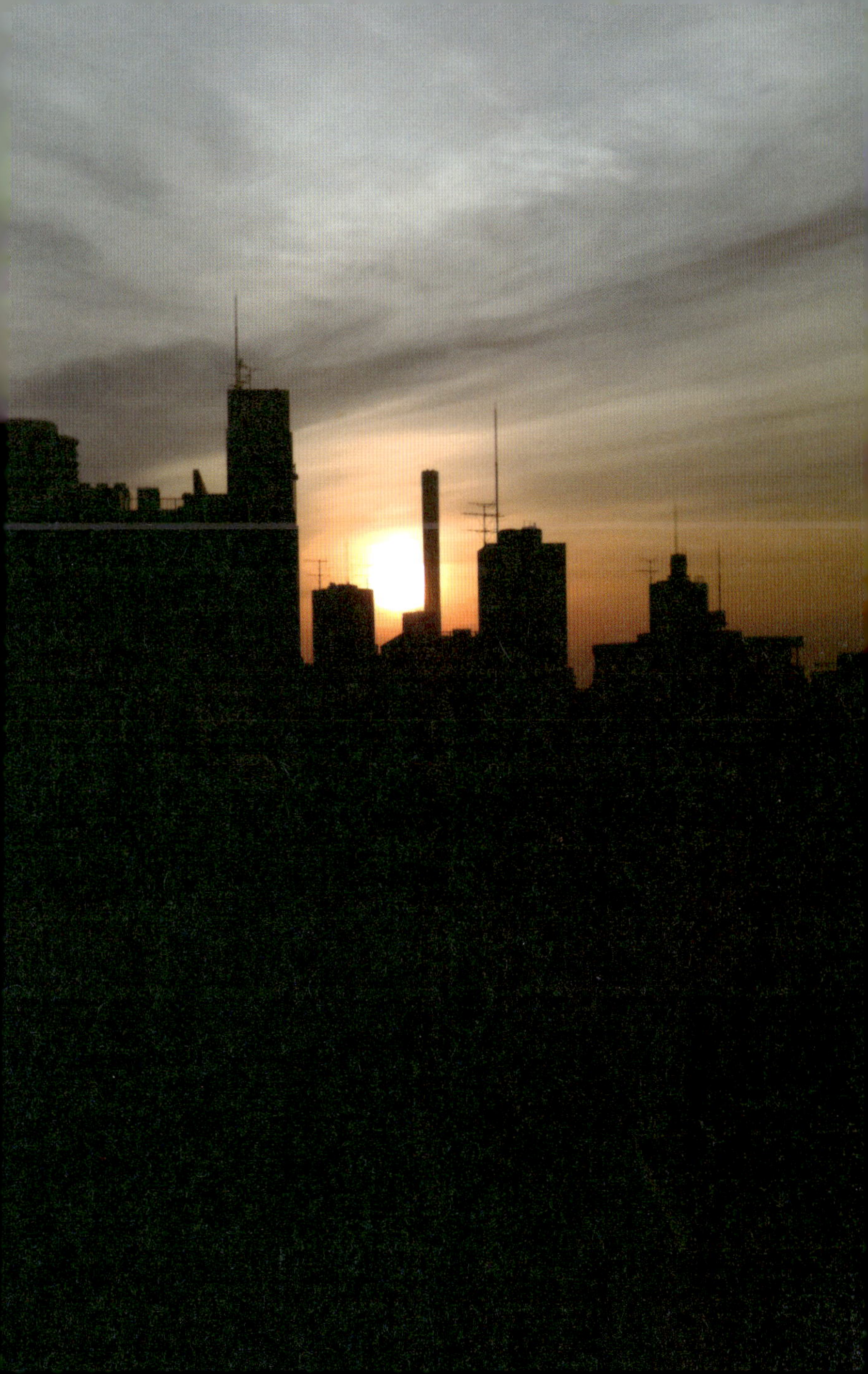

動けなくなること

振り返ってみると、「動けなくなること」が
この病気と戦うなかで一番キツイ試練だったと思う。

ソファの上で2時間、立ち上がろうとしてできなかったり。
ベッドで5時間、トイレに行きたくても、
ヘルパーを呼べなかったり。
サンドイッチを取ろうとして、頭が落ち、
テーブルの上でうつ伏せ状態で2時間動けなかったこともあった。
道ばたで倒れ、動けなくなったときは、
ようやく誰かが助けてくれるまで20分間、
仰向けの状態で過ごしたこともある。

すごく怖かったのは、自分自身の体が麻痺して、
僕の言うことを完全に聞かないこと。
心臓の鼓動が高まって、大量の汗をかき始める。

自分自身がヘンなマインドトリックみたいなものにかかって、ずっとそこから動けないんだって信じてしまう……。

そんなときは、いろいろなことを考えて自分を落ち着かせていた。
なにかひとつのことを集中して考えていたわけではないけど、
冷静さを保つために
哲学的なことや、感情的なことは、一切考えなかった。

逆に考えたのは、肉体的な満足のこと。
たとえばセックスのことだったり、背中を掻いたりすること。

確かにとても浅はかなんだけど、僕はパニックに陥ることを
阻止するために、そう考えるようになっていた。

みんなはそんなとき、どんなことを考えるんだろう。

Being Stuck...
Looking back, "being stuck" has been one of the toughest challenges of this disease. Stuck on the couch for two hours, fighting to stand up. Stuck in bed for five hours, needing to pee but struggling to call my helper. Stuck two hours face down on the table after I tried to pick up a sandwich. Stuck twenty minutes on my back in the middle of the street before somebody finally decided to help me get up.
It was scary to feel my body paralyzed and completely irresponsive to my demands. Your heart starts pounding and you start sweating profusely. **You know you won't be, but your mind somehow tricks you to believe that you'll be stuck there forever.**
During those times I thought about all kinds of things to stay calm. I won't get into the specifics of each thought, but to get my peace-of-mind I didn't think about philosophical or emotional shit. I found it in simple thoughts of physical satisfaction, ranging anywhere from sex to a simple scratch on the back. Call me shallow, but that's where my mind ended up keeping me from panicking and breaking down. I wonder where everybody else goes...

第二の人生

2011年11月30日(32歳の誕生日)午前2時、
気づいたら母親の腕のなかで過呼吸となり、
窒息しそうになっていた。
意識を失っては、取り戻すことの繰り返し。

次に記憶として残っているのは救急車のなか。
そして目が覚めると、ER(緊急救命室)にいた。
目を開けると担当医や看護師に囲まれていた。

僕が担当医に聞いた最初のひとこと。

「ここはどこ?」

よくテレビなんかで聞くセリフだけど、
実際に人間が意識を取り戻したとき、最初に思いつくのが
このことなんだなって実感した。

意識が戻るなり、医療的な、これからの治療手順の説明があった。

「とにかく、先生が正しいと思う方法で進めてください。
そして僕はなにをすべきか教えてください」

僕には、こう答えることしかできなかった。

翌朝、担当医は病室に入ってくるなり、

「藤田さん、20分病院に運ばれる
のが遅ければ命はなかったですよ。
Happy Birthday！」

僕はその後、3週間入院し、人工呼吸器とマスクとともに退院した。
言葉で伝えるは難しいけど、
「死」というものを少し実感した気がする。

感覚：冷たくてドライ
感情：悲しみもなく、恐れもない。
ただ「死ぬんだ……」という事実だけ。

「死」って人間のなかでもっとも大げさで、
ドラマティックにとらえられているコンセプトなのかもしれない。

これは残される人たちにとっては違うけど、
ただ、「逝く」人間にとってはとてもあっさりとしていて、
シンプルだ。

Second life
Novembar 30th, 2011 2:00am (my 32nd birthday), I was suffocating in my mom's arms. I was hyperventilating and in-and-out of consciousness. Before I knew it I was in an ambulance. Then the next moment I was in the ER. I opened my eyes and I was surrounded by doctors and nurses. The first thing I asked was "Where am I?" They said "the hospital, Jikei Hospital." The doctor started to explain all kinds of procedures that he recommended. All I said to him is "do everything you think is right and tell me what to do." Next morning, the doctor walked into the room and told me **I was 20 minutes away from not making it, and "happy birthday."** I stayed there for three weeks. I left the hospital with a respirator support machine and a mask, which I need to have next to me at all times to make sure I don't stop breathing.
It's hard to explain, but I did experience death a little bit. When I was slipping in-and-out of consciousness, I remember it was very cold and dry. There was no emotion, nothing was scary or sad, just the cold truth that I was dying. I now think that death is probably one of the most over-rated concepts. People have built it up to be something very dramatic. It may be so for the people who are left behind, but for the people who go, it's plain and simple.

いろいろな考えの整理をしている
途中ではあるが、
きっと「生」と「死」は
紙一重なんだ。

生きているからこそ、
今こう思う。
僕は生死の狭間で「死」を
少し騙せたのかもしれない。

だからこれからは、日常のなかで
「生きる」ことに対して
もっと楽しみを見つけていけるよう、
賢く生きていきたい。

There's a fine line between living and dying. I'm still trying to settle these thoughts in my mind. **I kind of feel that I cheated death.** Since then I've been trying to cheat more out of life every day.

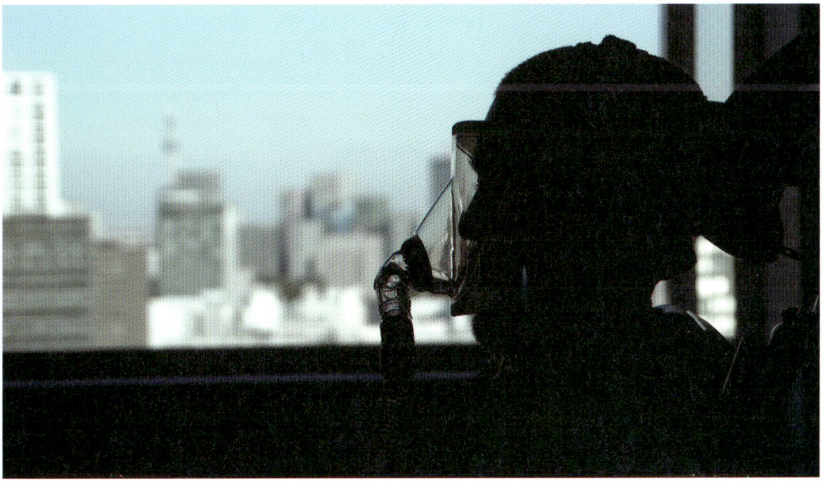

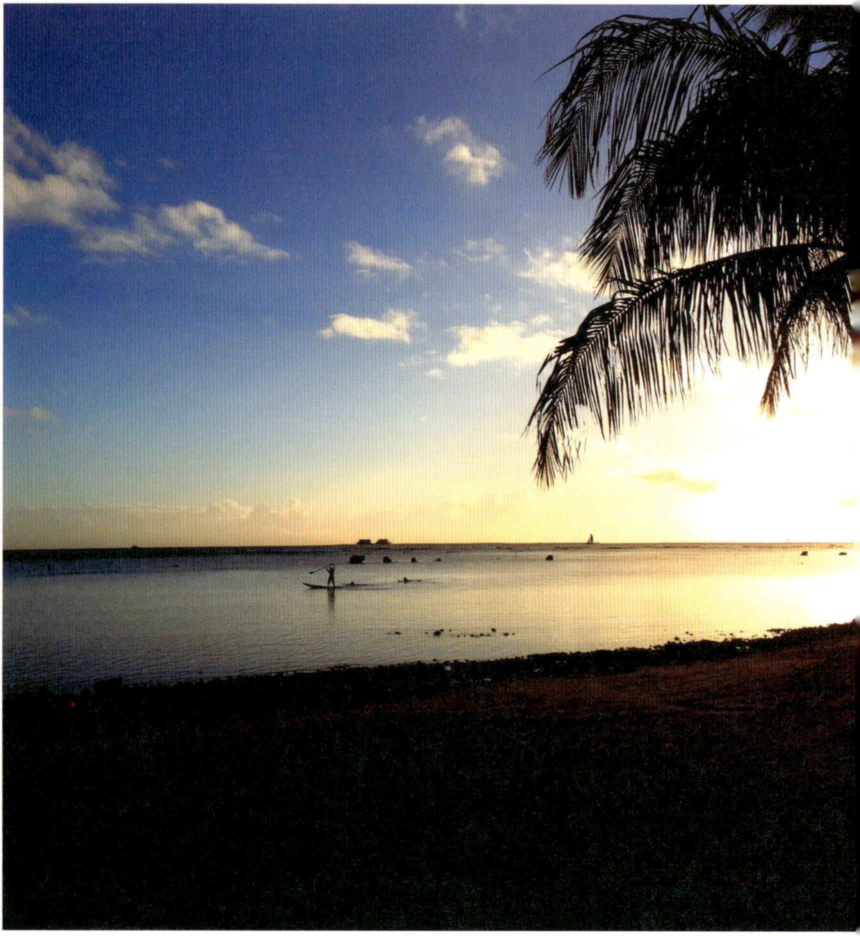

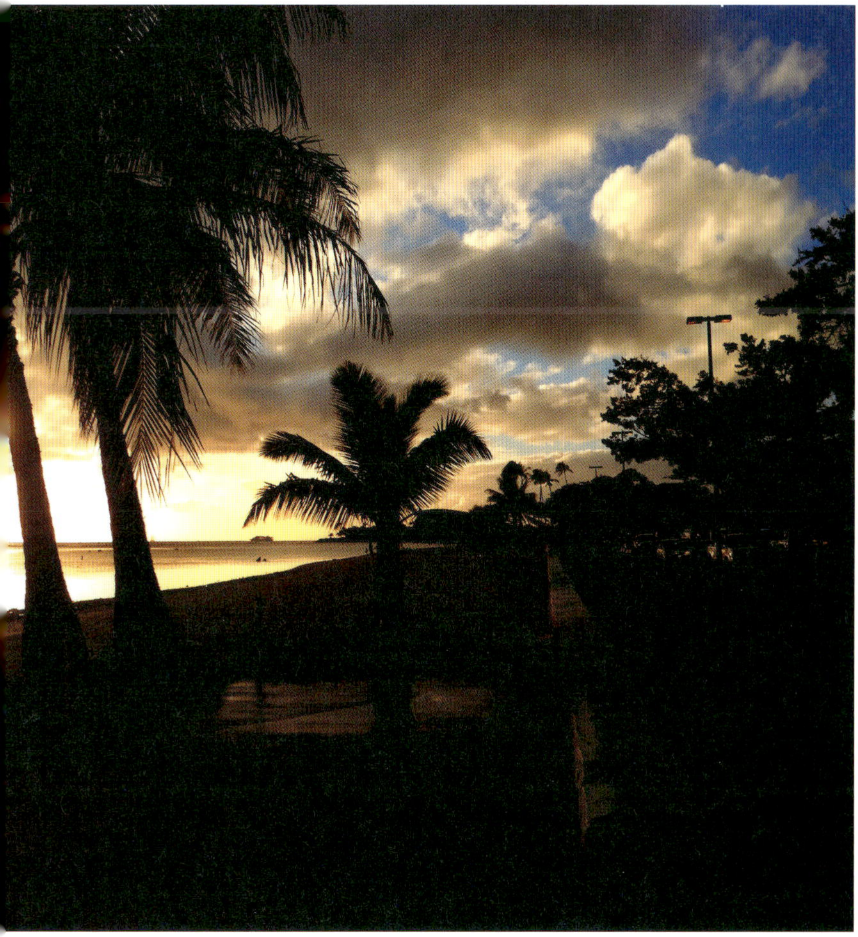

親友からもらった温かい言葉たち

1.「えっ、死ぬって知ってるんでしょ？」
友達が僕の残り時間がどれだけ少ないかを理由にし、
ビールを（？）飲ませようとした時の言葉。

2.「えっ、良かったじゃん！
　　もう歩かなくていいわけでしょ？」
友達が僕の新しい電動車椅子を見たとき、
物事をポジティブにとらえた一言。

3.「あら残念」
友達に診断の説明をする長いメールを書いたとき、
戻ってきた二言の返信。
気の利いた言葉が見つからなかったのだろう……。

おれ、いい友達いて良かったー‼
ｗｗ（'▽`）ノ

These are some of the beautiful words that have been given to me by friends:
1. "You know you're gonna die right?"
When a friend was trying to persuade me to drink, he found it in his heart to point out how short my time left may be.
2. "Oh that's great, so you don't have to walk now!!"
When a friend saw me in my new electronic wheelchair, she saw the positive side of things.
3. "Oh bummers."
When a friend replied with two words to my long e-mail explaining my diagnosis... I guess he was...speechless.
Oh am I so lucky to have such wonderful friends!!

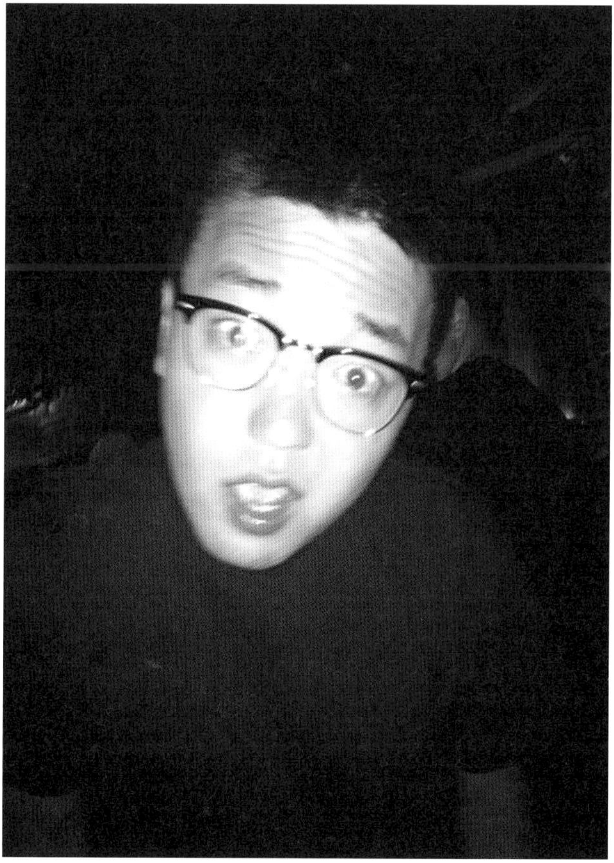

テクノロジー

最初は、人工呼吸器を夜だけ装着していたが、
徐々につける時間が延びていった。

頼れば頼るほど必要になると思い、
なるべく使わないように頑張った。
けど無理。半年ぐらいしたら一日中付けてた。

顔全体を覆うプラスチックのマスクなので、
ストラップは痛いし、声は聞こえないし、
食べるのも２、３口食べたらまた装着しなくてはならない。

大変だけど、毎晩友達に食事をこぼされながら楽しんでいた。
声は喉にマイクを装着し、小さいスピーカーを通して会話していた。

今は、極力人間らしく生きるのにテクノロジーは欠かせない。

Technology
Initially, I put on the breathing apparatus only at night.
Gradually, I had to have it on for longer periods of time.
The more you rely on it, the more you think you need it so I tried to stay off it as much as possible.
But six months later I had it on 24/7.
The plastic mask covered the entire face.
The straps dug in my head and hurt.
People couldn't hear my voice.
With food, I would take off the mask for a couple of bites and quickly put it back on again.
It was difficult but it was alright. My friends and I would laugh every night as they helped me to eat, spilling here and there.
I had a microphone around my throat and was able to talk through tiny speakers.
Technology is allowing me to live like a human being.

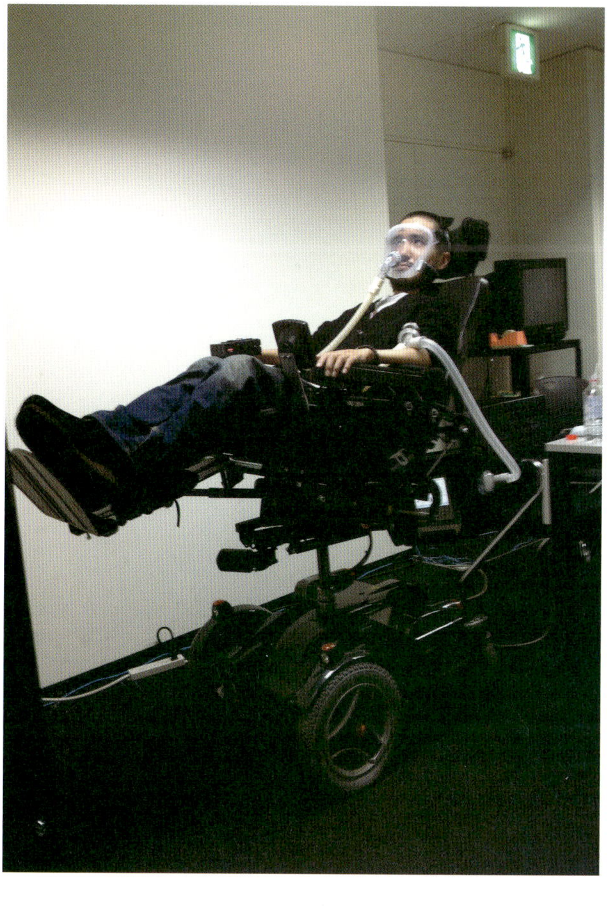

涙が出るとき

気づけば半年以上も泣いていない。
これってヘンなのかな。

前はよく泣いていた。
母親の泣いている姿を見たときとか、
動けないことにイライラしたときとか、
自分がかわいそうに思えたときだとか。

このような出来事は、ここ最近も起きているけど、
泣けていない。慣れてきているのかな？
それとも、いつか一気に押し寄せて崩れちゃうのかな？

「もうどうでもいい」わけではないけど、
泣くほどのことではないと思えてきた。

要は、この状態が「普通」になってきた。
この病気を持って生まれてきたかのように感じる。
もうすでに病気前の人生がどうだったかを忘れ始めている。

治療法が見つかることを想像すると、
あまりにも非現実的で、めまいがする。
ALSがもう自分の現実になっている。

「ヒロがALSだと診断された」は、もう過去の話だ。
「ヒロはALSと生きている」が「最新の」ニュースなのかも
しれない（さすがにこの言葉を口にするのには慣れない）。

今後、価値のあるニュースは「治療」だけなのかもしれない。そのときが来たら、久しぶりに泣けると思う。

Forgot how to cry...
I haven't cried in 6 months. Is that weird? I mean, I used to cry quite a bit. Every time I saw my mom cry, or when I got frustrated from not being able to move or times when I just felt sorry for myself. All of this has continued to happen in the past 6 months but I haven't cried. Maybe I'm just getting used to it? Or maybe I'm just gonna break down someday? Not that I don't care...it's just not worth crying about anymore.
It's all become normal, I guess. I feel as though I was born with it. I'm already forgetting what life was like before. The thought of a cure and returning to that life is so overwhelming and unreal it makes me feel nauseous. This is my life now. "Hiro diagnosed with ALS" is not the news anymore. I hate to admit it but I guess I am at the "Hiro living with ALS" stage (fuck I hate saying that).
Now, only the cure will be newsworthy.
And that's probably when I'll be able to cry again.

イライラ vs. ありがたみ

イライラがピークに達することがある。
自分のペースで食べられない。かゆいところをかけない。
自分の好きなように自分のケツも拭けない。

右手を上げてと頼むと左手を上げられたり、
動かない足を間違えて踏まれたり、
ストローの入った飲み物をなぜかめちゃくちゃ口に近づけられ、
ストローが喉の奥に刺さったり。

ALS＝「我慢」とも言えるだろう。
だけど、わかっている。

**同時にそれだけ多くの人に
支えられていること。
痛いほど感謝している。
それは間違いない。**

だけど、ときにはイライラが勝っちゃう日もある。
本当に申し訳ない。

Frustration vs. Appreciation

My frustration level has been at an all-time high lately...
I'm sick of this shit.
I can't eat at my own pace, scratch where I want, or even wipe my own ass how I want it to be wiped.
When I ask to have my right hand raised, people usually raise my left.
People kick my feet by mistake all the time.
For some reason, they bring my drink too close to my face, stabbing the back of my throat with the straw.
I think it's safe to say ALS = Patience.
Yet I also recognize that all of these experiences illustrate the number of people that support my life today. I couldn't be more appreciative of this...but some days my "frustration" wins...
For those who have seen such days...I'm truly sorry.

母の日

呼吸がかなりつらくなり、
出せる声の音量もどんどん小さくなっていった。
そんななか、気づいた。
これ、声を出して話す最後の言葉たちかも。

「あなたなら最後に何を声にしますか？」

深い質問だと思った。けど、迷わず答えが出た。
マザコンとでもなんとでも呼んでくれ。

「ママ、ありがとう」だ。

「親孝行どころか迷惑かけっぱなし。
なかなか休ませてあげられなくてゴメン。
いつまでも俺の母親でいてくれてありがとう」

だね。

Mother's Day
It's getting tough to breathe.
My voice is getting smaller and smaller.
That's when I realized,
These words might be one of the last that I voice out.
"What would you say with your last words?"
I thought this was a deep philosophical question.
However I found that it was the easiest to answer.
My last words would be **"Mom, Thank you."**
"I'm supposed to be taking care of you, and yet you still do.
I'm sorry I'm not allowing you to rest...
Thank you for being my mother."

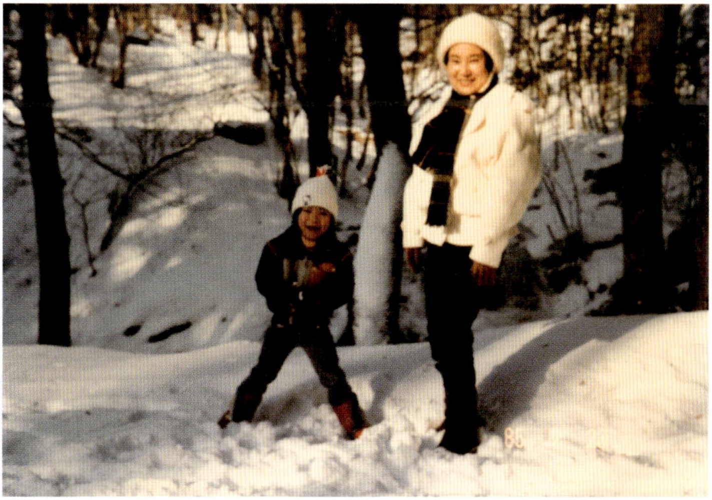

日本国にマジで死ぬ？
生きる？　と聞かれた……はーっ？

自発呼吸ができなくなっても、気管切開すれば、
事故がないかぎり、10年も20年も生き続けられる。

だが、その間、ALSの進行は止まらない。
途中、諦めたくても、一度気管切開したら、
はずすことは法律上認められていない。

そのため、約70％のALS患者は、
気管切開しないで「死」を選ぶ。

恐怖はもちろん、周りへの金銭的、精神的、
身体的な負担・迷惑を恐れてのことだと聞く。

**もし、途中で呼吸器をはずす選択肢が認められれば、
ほぼ全員、気管切開するのではないでしょうか？**

ということは、今の法律、人を殺してませんか？
もっと父親と「会話」したかった娘……
母親の手を握ってあげたかった息子……
この法律で無理な選択を迫られ、無念。
法律、規制に化けてる殺人、残酷すぎます。

Murder disguised as laws and regulations

As long as there are no accidents, ALS patients can potentially live for 10, 20 years if we get a tracheotomy. However, ALS never stops attacking the limited motor neurons we have left. Even if it finishes off everything, including your eyes, and you can't take it anymore, if we choose the tube then we're never allowed to take it off. Euthanasia is not legal in Japan. This is why approx. 70% of ALS patients choose "death" over a tracheotomy. Reasons vary. Fear of what's ahead, and burdening loved ones financially, emotionally, physically, etc.
If we were given that option, to take it off, don't you think almost 100% of people would choose to try it out?
If this is true, doesn't this mean that the law is killing people?
The daughter who wanted to have more "talks" with dad...
The son who wanted to hold his mom's hand for just a little longer...
They are forced to choose the impossible...it's murder disguised as laws and regulations... it's simply evil...

頑張ります

「頑張って」とよく言われる。
その半分の方は直後に、「頑張ってじゃないよね……」と
気を遣ってくださる。
心苦しい。

応援してくれているのに、罪悪感を感じさせちゃってる。

僕が思うには、正解です。
「頑張って」でいいのです。

「他人事のように言うなよ」とか
「言われなくても頑張ってるよ」とか言っている人は、
まだまだ頑張れるんだと思う。
だからひねくれちゃうんじゃない？

僕にはそんな余裕はありません。
僕はみんなの応援をありがたく受けとめ、頑張ります。
イェイ。

I'll give it my best

People often tell me "ganbatte" (keep trying, or stay strong) but immediately after, half of them say, "I'm sorry if that's not the right thing to say." They're trying to be polite.
This kills me.
I'm making them feel bad for expressing their support for me.
If you ask me, they are not wrong.
Ganbatte is correct.
Those who say, "Yeah, like you know what it's like" or "I AM giving my best, what more do you want from me?" still have a loooong way to go.
That's why they have the energy to be cynical.
I, on the other hand, am at my limits.
So I will thankfully accept any words of support and encouragement.

ヘルパー

一時期、毎日のように自分でヘルパーの研修をしてた。
技術をもったヘルパーを探すのが大変。
これは国にどうにかしてもらいたい。

巨体なのに超弱い人。
爪は長くいつもひっかかれ、足は踏まれ。
暑いのか僕に汗を垂らすが、なぜかシャツ二枚にタートルネック。
おチンチンを触るのが怖いのか、尿瓶で突っつきながら
なかに入れようとしたり。

ベッドに座らせるのに「失礼します、失礼します」と
40回ぐらい言いながら結局できなかった人には、
さすがにその場で帰ってもらった。

できるヘルパーは他の患者が放さない。
本当のヘルパーが足りない。
ヘルパーの重要性を理解して、
給料や資格の難易度を
高める必要がある。

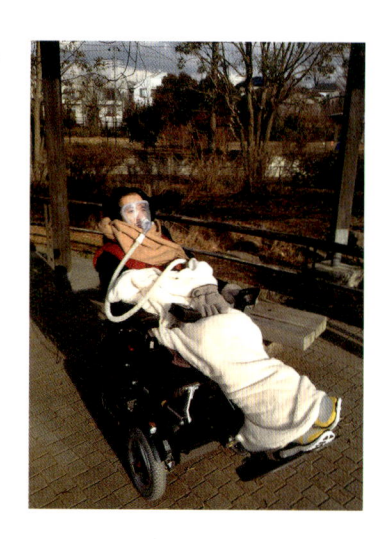

神経質でせっかちな自分には、
今まで自分の手や足や声でできたことを、
すべて他人にやってもらうのに慣れるのは、
想像以上に大変なことだ。

きっと、一生慣れないまま終わると思う。
人間は、そうやって生きるようにできていないからね。

今は、2年一緒にいてくれているヘルパーが多いから、
ある程度意思疎通できているが、
いつ、誰がどうなるかわからないから、不安は消えない。

Helper/Caretaker

In the beginning, I was training helpers myself every day.
It's difficult to find a skilled helper.
This is something the government must deal with.
A huge helper, but weak as hell.
Another with long nails leaving scratch marks,
They all step on my feet.
Another who sweats like crazy, dripping that shit on me but for some reason he always wore three layers with a turtleneck.
Another who was scared to touch my penis so she used the urinal every time to poke and try to stick it in. Lady! It ain't gonna bite! Not you!
There was one helper who apologized about 40 times BEFORE he tried to sit me up on the bed. And after all that, he still failed …I had to send him home on the spot…get out…
Patients don't let go of skilled helpers.
Able helpers are really hard to come by.
There needs to be a system in place that correctly acknowledges the value and importance of this profession, in terms of salary and the levels for qualification.

I've always been very particular and impatient.
It was more difficult than you think to let go and have others do everything for you.
I probably will never get used to it.
Because people aren't made to live like that.
Now, my helpers have been with me for two years so I feel relatively comfortable with them. But anything could happen to anyone at any given moment so that insecurity/anxiety remains…

原発

原子力発電所が及ぼした被害は、わかっている。
二度と許されるものではない。
社会に「反対するべき空気」が流れているのもわかる。
ニュースを見ていると、今までにない反対運動が起きていて
「民間が国を動かしてる感」が頼もしいのもわかる。

だけど、もし、反対している人やその家族が
ALSと診断されたらどうなるだろう？
意見、変わるのかな？　コロッて……。

原子力発電所がないと、安定的に電力を供給できないらしい。
停電は、私のように人工呼吸器／補助器を必要としている者には
恐ろしい状況だ。

バッテリー残量がなくなれば、呼吸ができなくなる。
(呼吸困難→尿漏れ→母の悲鳴→救急車→入院→
喉に穴を空けて呼吸器を付ける→医療費がかかる……etc)
簡単に受け入れられるリスクではない。
なので、自分である程度準備をしている。

けど、これも少数派だから「いろんな立場がある」で
片づけられちゃうのかね。

Nuclear Power Plant

I understand the tragedy the nuclear power plants have caused, and it's not something that can be forgiven twice.
I also understand the general sentiment of our society, to get rid of the plants.
The news show people protesting like never before and it feels good to see "the people moving the nation."
However, what would happen if a protester or one of their family members were to be diagnosed with ALS? Would their views and opinions change? Just like that?
Apparently, if there are no nuclear power plants, the likelihood for blackouts increases.
This is a devastating situation for someone like me who depends on respirators and other devices to live.
If the battery runs out, my life runs out.
This means I suffocate, piss in my pants, my mom cries, ambulance arrives, I'm hospitalized, I open a hole in my throat to be connected to an oxygen tank, medical bills, etc.
These are not risks I can easily accept even though I obviously prepare for the worst to some extent.
Then again, I guess this is a minority opinion so will be brushed off as an acceptable loss...
Shiiiiieeeeet...

GOAL

サッカーが好きなんだけど、ここ5、6年やっていなかった。
いつも「仕事が忙しい」とか、「二日酔い」が理由だった。
サッカーを楽しめることが当然だと思っていたことを、
今、後悔している。

今はこの写真を自分のゴールとして部屋に飾っている。
いつかまたボールを蹴れるように。

GOAL
I've always loved soccer.
But I haven't played for the past 5~6 years because I always had excuses like "I'm too busy with work" or "I'm too hung over."
I regret taking the joys of soccer for granted.
Now I have this picture up as my life's goal......
to kick a ball around again someday.......

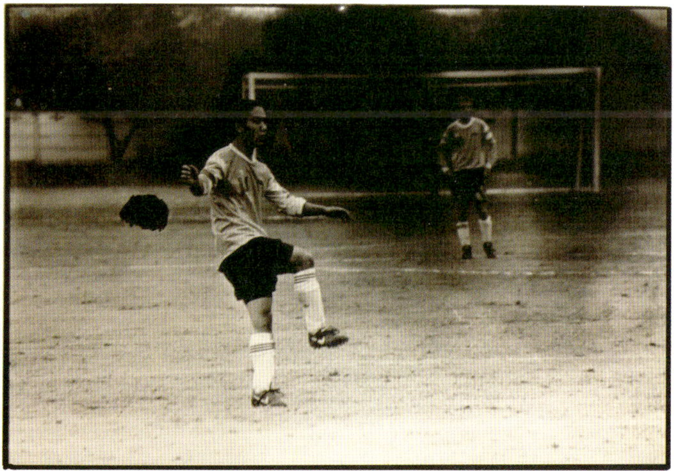

話せる価値

久しぶりに、入院ではなく外来受診のため病院に行ったときのこと。
受診を待つ患者たちが前のめりになって
こっちを興味深く見るなか、病院を進んだ。

まず採血。看護師さんが二人がかりでやってくれた。
そしたら、奇妙な経験をした。看護師が母親とヘルパーに、

「どちらの腕でも大丈夫ですか？」

と尋ね、親が、

「はい」

と答えると、看護師が僕の左腕を取り、
「ここ」と言いながら左手の甲を取り、
聞き慣れた「チクッとしま～す」もなしに刺され、
聞き慣れてる「抜きま～す」もなしに抜かれ、
親とヘルパーに「終わりで～す。ありがとうございました」と言い、
僕と一度も目が合わずに終わった。

体が動かなくてしゃべれないと、こんなもんかね。
気を悪くしているわけではないが、

「新しい……ワイルド……」

と、思った。
この先の「モノ扱い」される生活が、徐々に姿を現してきたぜぃ。

The value of speech

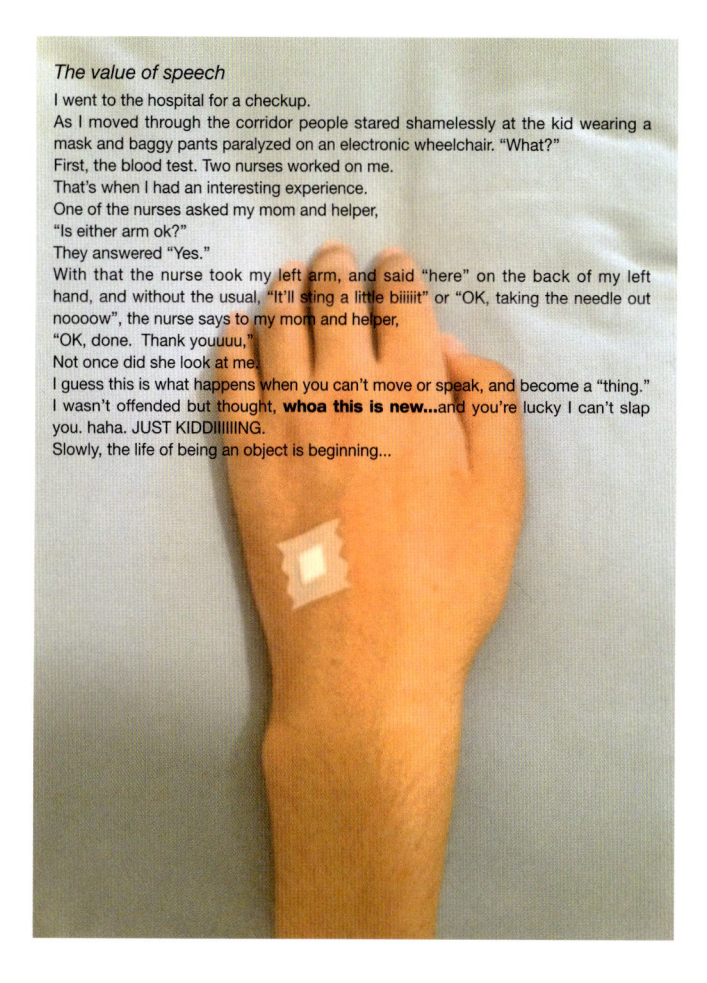

I went to the hospital for a checkup.
As I moved through the corridor people stared shamelessly at the kid wearing a mask and baggy pants paralyzed on an electronic wheelchair. "What?"
First, the blood test. Two nurses worked on me.
That's when I had an interesting experience.
One of the nurses asked my mom and helper,
"Is either arm ok?"
They answered "Yes."
With that the nurse took my left arm, and said "here" on the back of my left hand, and without the usual, "It'll sting a little biiiiit" or "OK, taking the needle out noooow", the nurse says to my mom and helper,
"OK, done. Thank youuuu,"
Not once did she look at me.
I guess this is what happens when you can't move or speak, and become a "thing."
I wasn't offended but thought, **whoa this is new...**and you're lucky I can't slap you. haha. JUST KIDDIIIIING.
Slowly, the life of being an object is beginning...

A burden

The words I hear so often when watching Japanese documentaries about ALS, "I don't want to be a burden."
Honestly, since the diagnosis, not a day has gone by that I don't think about how much of a burden I must be to everybody around me.
I have to rely on others for every-single thing, even breathing.
So, I must be, I know I am.
But I have to keep it positive. The patient, has to accept that a certain level of trouble to others is a given, it is now a fact of life.
But if you're too selfish, people walk away.
So there needs to be a fine balance.
As much as I find it difficult and scary, I tell myself
"I'm not going to be afraid to be a burden."
Sorry… I hope you can forgive me.

迷惑

ALSについての日本のドキュメンタリーを見るとよく聞く言葉、
「迷惑かけたくないから」。

僕も正直、ALSと診断されてから、
「俺の存在って迷惑なのかな」とほぼ毎日考えてしまう。

そりゃ、すべてのことを周りに頼らないといけなくなると、
そう感じるのは仕方がない。
そのうえ、事実、迷惑だとは思う。

しかし、極力そう考えないようにしないと、やってられなくなる。
ヘンな話、「ある程度の迷惑をかけるのは当たり前」と
患者自身が受け入れないといけない。

とはいえ、わがまますぎると人は離れていく。
絶妙なバランスが求められる。
ちなみに、僕は、気が引けるし、怖いし、心苦しいけど、

「迷惑をかけるのだけは恐れない！」

……ようにしてる。お許しを。

我慢

たしか、北島三郎さんが、昔テレビ番組で言ってた。

「我慢できる
我慢は
我慢じゃない」

昔から折れそうになると、
この言葉を思い出してきた。
これからです。

Endurance
Whenever I'm close to breaking,
I remember the words of Japanese musician Saburo Kitajima.
"Enduring what you can endure is not true endurance."
It starts from here…

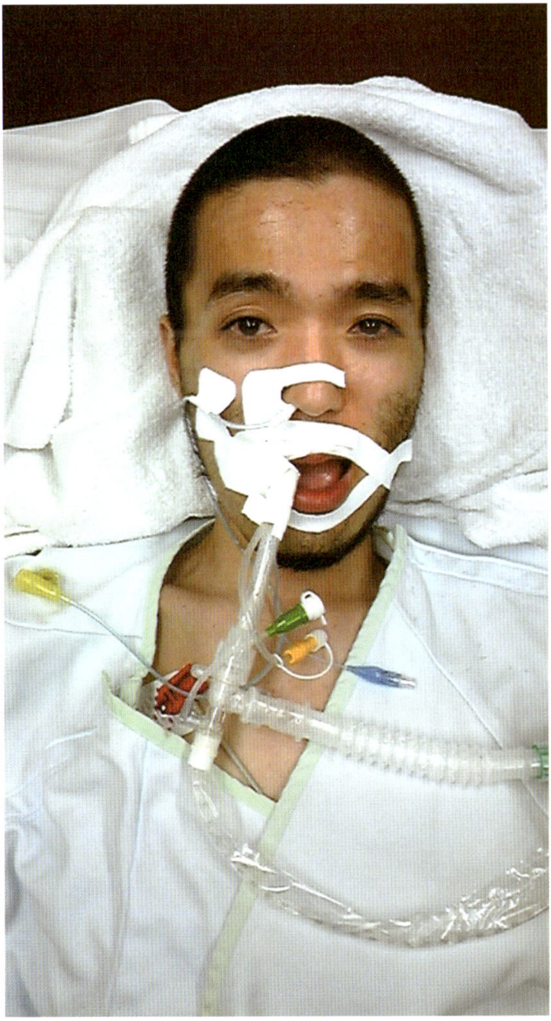

勇気と諦め

自分の体の動きをひとつひとつ、
3年かけてゆっくりと取り上げられるのを見てきた。
だからかもしれない。
生活環境を変えろ、手放せと言われると、
死守モードに入ってしまう。

退職？　実家へ帰る？　気管切開？　ポータブルトイレ？　吸引？

ざっけんな！　まだまだ！

それはぜってぇあげねぇ……と、考える前に言ってる。

受け入れて対処したほうが楽なのは知っているけど。
どんな小さいことでも手放すのを受け入れちゃうと、
自分は生きるのを諦め始めているんじゃないかと焦ってしまう。

周りに迷惑をかけているのは知っているし、申し訳ないけど、
どこまでが受け入れる勇気で、どこまでが諦めなのかが
見えにくくなってる。

Courage or giving up

Over the past 3 years, I have watched all movement of my body slowly being taken away from me... one by one. This is probably why when I'm told to let go of something I instinctively prepare to defend it with my life. Quit my job? Go back to my parents? Get a tracheotomy? Get a portable toilet? Use the suction machine? Before I even consider it I react with a **"Hell No!" Not yet!** I'm not giving you that... I know it's easier if I learn to accept it but... Every time I let go of something from my previous life, regardless of how small it may be, I worry I may be getting that much closer to giving up. It makes me tense... I know this attitude is a burden and a pain in the ass to the many people around me. I'm sorry for that, but I'm confused as hell right now. I'm not sure where to draw the line between the courage of accepting/letting go, versus giving up.

必ずその日は来る

「治ったな」「待ってたぞ」「お帰り」
って言われるとき……。

腕を動かした、歩いた、人工呼吸器を外して深呼吸した瞬間。
大笑いした、大泣きした瞬間。
食べ物、刈られた芝生、アンタの体臭を匂う瞬間。
もう一度のチャンス、命を頂ける日……。

That day will come...

When you can tell me,
"You're cured," "we've missed you," "welcome back"...that moment,
I move my arms, walk, take off my mask and breathe...
I laugh out loud... cry out loud...
I smell food, freshly cut grass, your B.O...that day, I'm given a second chance... a second life...

毎日

発病して2年近く、一人暮らしを続けていた。
ヘルパーに来てもらえる時間が
17時間しか認められていなかったため、
僕の家に毎晩、誰かしら友達が来てくれた。

夕方から23時まで、食材を買ってきて食事を作ってくれるか、
出前をとって、食事介助もしてくれ、
喉が詰まったらカフアシスト(排痰の補助)もして、
尿瓶を当てることまで。
トイレに担いでいってケツを拭いてくれたコトもある。

しまいには共通のカレンダーをネット上に作り、
その日の当番を埋めてくれた。
どうしても誰も来られない日は、一年に数日。
そういうときは兄や母に来てもらった。

「これもトレンドだからずっとは続かないよ」と、
自分に言い聞かせていた。が、続いた。

人生一の財産・宝物の重みをあらためて、痛いほど感じた。

僕ほど友達に恵まれている人はいない。

Every day

For two years after my diagnosis, I lived alone.
Insurance only covered for 17 hours of caretakers each day so my friends came over to my place EVERY night to take care of me.
From early evening to 11PM, they went grocery shopping and cooked, or ordered some delivery, help me eat, or do the cough assist machine if something got caught in my throat.
Some assisted me with the urinal and one even carried me to the toilet and wiped my ass...
They made an online calendar so someone would always be here, almost every night.
There were just a few days a year when nobody could make it.
At those times, my brother or my mom filled in.
I told myself,
"This is probably a phase or a trend, it won't last."
But it did.
I am painfully aware of this invaluable treasure of mine.
Nobody is blessed more than me when it comes to friends.

また死にそうになった、
2013年1月5日

あぶなかったーっ！
あぶなすぎて声を失った。原因は肺炎。

一通りの儀式はおこなった。
ムセが続き、吸引しまくり、窒息、尿漏れ、気絶、救急車、
家族、ヘルパーたちの恐怖、死と会話……。

ICUで目覚めた。
喉に穴ができて、
ICUから普通の病棟に解放された。
気管切開、しました。

体力的にも精神的にも痛い。
けど、皆に「応援ありがとう」
と言いたいです。

気管切開・延命して、
前に進む理由・勇気をくれて、
本当にありがとうございます。

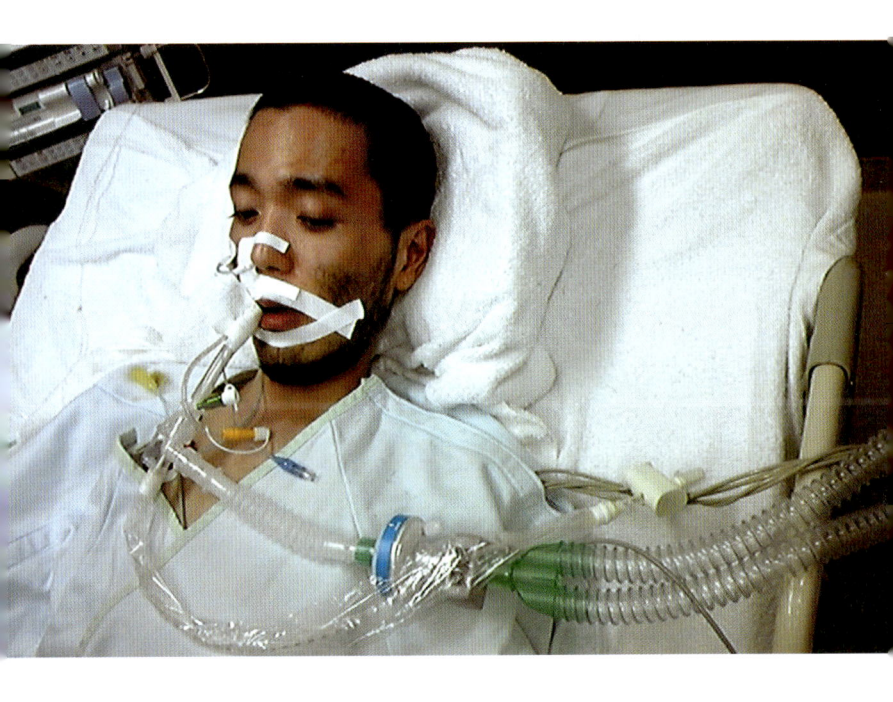

Almost died again... January 5th, 2013

That was way too close...

Actually, so close that I ended up losing my voice...pneumonia got me...

went through the routine again... constant choking/vacuuming flem, suffocate, piss in pants, slowly lose consciousness, ambulance, terrified family, docs, nurses, helpers, ending in another conversation with death...

Woke up in the ICU...

Just got out yesterday with a hole in my throat...

A tracheotomy...

It hurts, emotionally and physically but just wanted to thank you for all of your support.

Thank you for always giving me the motivation and courage to keep living.

気管切開

それは、鼻と口を使わずに呼吸できることに慣れ、
パニックをおこさないこと（顔が水中でも呼吸できる）。

それは、人がハンバーガーを食べて、
コーラを飲んでいる姿を見て空腹を満たすこと。

それは、世間話、冗談、口論などからは手を引くこと。

それは、「生き続ける」と腹をくくること。

Tracheostomy

Is about getting used to not breathing from mouth or nose and not panicking about it.
My face can be under water and still breathe.
Is about trying to feel full through watching people munch on their hamburgers and gulp down their Coke.
Is about letting go of the small talk/jokes/debates/etc.
Is about making a commitment to keep on living.

胃瘻栄養チューブ
（いろう）

胃に直接食物や水分を送る、
胃瘻をつけることになった。

最初の日。
誰かに指をおなかに刺し込まれ、
いじくりまわされる感じ。
笑ったり、咳をすると、
怪我をしてるアバラを殴られる痛み。
食事のためにチューブをつなげたり、
はずすたびに体内の何かを
引き出される感じ。

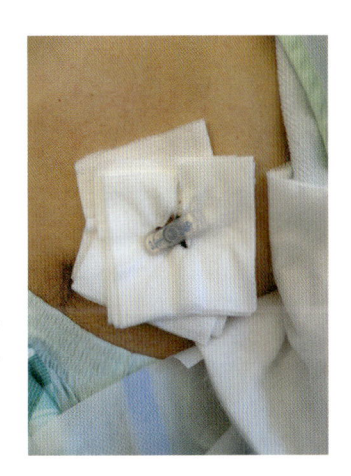

「我慢。すぐ治る。慣れるから」

……うん……やかましいわ。

Gastrostomy feeding tube

The first day...
It feels like somebody stabbing their finger in your stomach and sometimes twisting it, and somebody punching you in the ribs every time you laugh or cough.
Every time they put on/take off the tube from my peg, it feels like they're pulling out my insides...
"Don't worry Hiro, you'll get used to it"... ummm... stfu.

狂いそう

絶対、勝つ！
って言いながら死んだ人どれぐらいいるの？

奇跡は起きる！
って亡くなった人にどんな奇跡おきたの？

絶対諦めない！
って言いながら「もう殺してくれ」と祈る人はどれぐらい？

俺なら耐えられる！
って言って耐えられた人いるの？

てかこの場合、耐えるってなに？
これは全部向き合わないといけない。
ただ、もしその日が来たら「FUCK ALS」と言う
勇気があることを願う。

I'm gonna go crazy
"I'm gonna win!"
How many people died saying that?
"Miracles happen!"
What miracle happened to the dead?
"I'm not giving up!"
But how many people died begging for mercy?
"I can handle this!"
But I know not even the strongest can.
Actually, what does "handling this" mean in my case?
These are all realities I must face...
Either way, if that day comes, I pray I will have the courage to look at it straight in its eyes and say "FUCK ALS"...

交換しよっか？

あなたにこれを経験してもらいたいとは少しも思わない。
ただ、もしあなたも捕まったとしたら、
これをたまに言いたくなる気持ち、わかると思う。

おまえとおまえのつまんねー生活への愚痴や言い訳、
もう散々……正直、クソくらえ。

おまえにはその状況をどうにかする選択肢があるからこそ
その愚痴や言い訳を吐ける。
その出来事に参加することさえ取り上げられたとき、
さっきまで愚痴ってたことが有り難いことに聞こえてくるはずだよ。

選択肢があるなら ペラペラしゃべってねーで 黙って解決しろよ!! タコ。

ダメだ。俺、メッチャ嫉妬してる……。

Wanna trade?

I would never wish this upon you, but if it got you, you would understand the urge to say this...
Fuck you and your complaints and excuses for your sorry ass day. You just complain because you have an option to do something about it.
But when the ability to merely participate in that category of what you're complaining about is jeopardized, trust me, what you were just crying about will seem like a blessing. **So if you do have that option, stop talking so much, wasting your breath and man the fuck up! Do something about it!**
Damn, am I jealous of you...

昔は肉がついてた

もしできることが
あるなら、
今やるべき。

ALSにここまで運動神経をやられるのに2〜3年かかった。
昔はかなり運動しまくった。
けど、いまや1ミリも動かない。
全部取り返す日、待ってます。

I had sexy legs, I swear!
All I can say to you is, if you can do it, do it now.
It took ALS a couple years to kill my motor-neurons to this state.
I used to be athletic. Now not the slightest movement.
Looking forward to taking it all back.

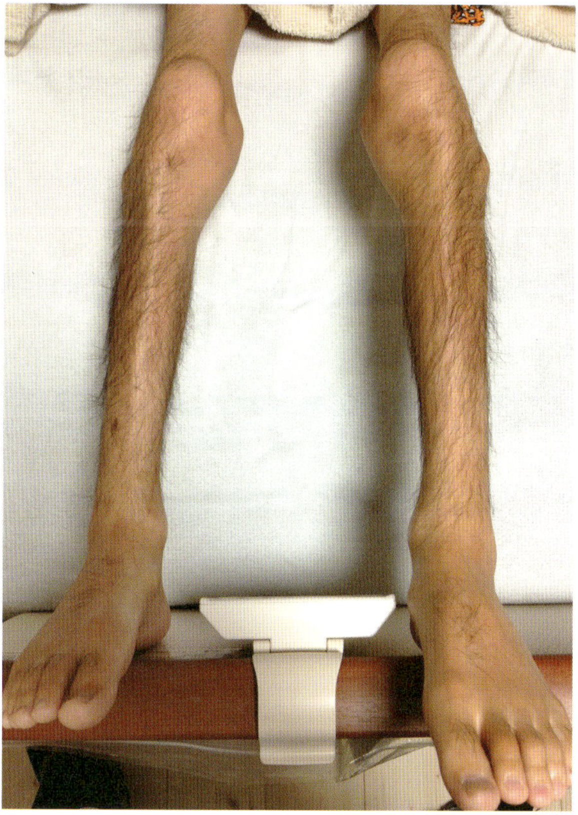

ロパク

僕と会話するにはロパクを読まなきゃならない。
面白い経験。完璧に読み取れる人もいる。
信じられないほどランダムな人もいる。

聞こえてるフリをする人、必死な人、
自分が聞きたいことしか聞こえない人、
逆に聞きたくないことしか聞こえない人、
超時間がかかる人、ただ手を握る人。

イライラする？　当たり前。

けど、あなたに対してじゃないことは覚えていてほしい。

病気との闘いの一環なだけ。

Lip read

People have to lip read to communicate with me.
It's interesting. Some people read spot on.
Some are unbelievably random.
Some pretend to understand.
Some are determined to.
Some guess what they want to hear.
Some what they don't.
Some take time.
Some just hold my hand.
Frustrating? Of course.
But pls remember, it's not at you.
It's just another part of my fight against the disease.

復興も治験も

知識、技術はすごい発展してるのに……。
あとは実現だけじゃないのかよ？

自分に理解できない難しい問題があるのはわかる。
けど、スピードを遅くしている大きな原因は
研究者・政治家の経営戦略・責任問題・勇気などだと思う。

これは復興にも言える。

患者も被害者も怖がってないよ。進めて……。

「100の言葉より1の行動」
by 安倍総理……たのみまっせ。

政府・研究者さま、「責任問題」でプロセスを遅らせないで。
そもそもの、その仕事の「責任」を感じてプロセスを速めてください。
「明日」では、もう一日遅いのです。

Recovery efforts and clinical trials
We have the knowledge, the technology…isn't it just action now?
I know that there are probably some difficult issues that I wouldn't understand.
But I get the feeling that a major factor causing the lack of speed is the management strategy, liability issues, and courage of the researchers and the politicians.
Same can be said for the recovery effort in Tohoku.
Patients and victims are NOT scared. Just MOVE it forward…
"1 action over 100 words," by PM Abe…you said it sir. Let's go.
The government and researchers please don't let responsibility issues slow the process down.
If anything, please embrace the responsibility of your roles and expedite the process.
"Tomorrow" is already one day too late.

風呂

昔は風呂で本を読むぐらい風呂が好きだった。
病気になって最後に入ったとき、
出られずのぼせ死にそうになったのを覚えてる。

久しぶりに入れて気持ちよかったー。
疲れたけど。
きわどい写真、ちょっとだけよ。

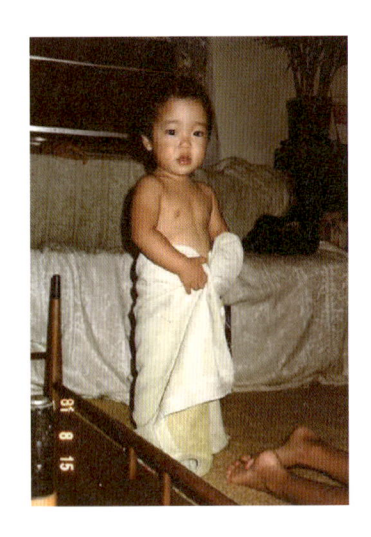

Bath
I used to enjoy relaxing and reading books while taking a bath.
The last time, I remember getting stuck, couldn't get out, almost boiling to death.
It's been a while… damn it felt good.
Enjoy my sexy pics.

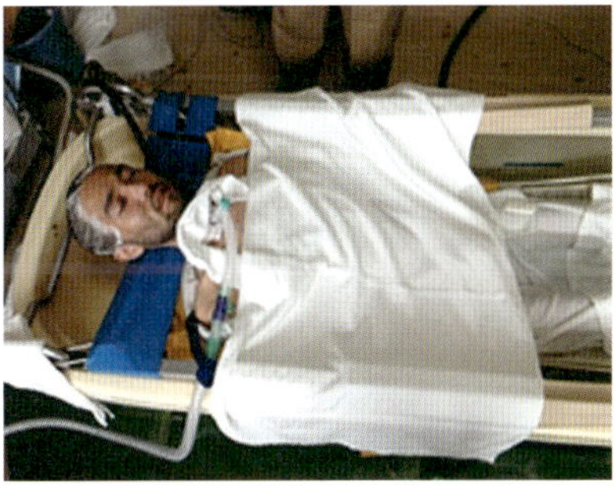

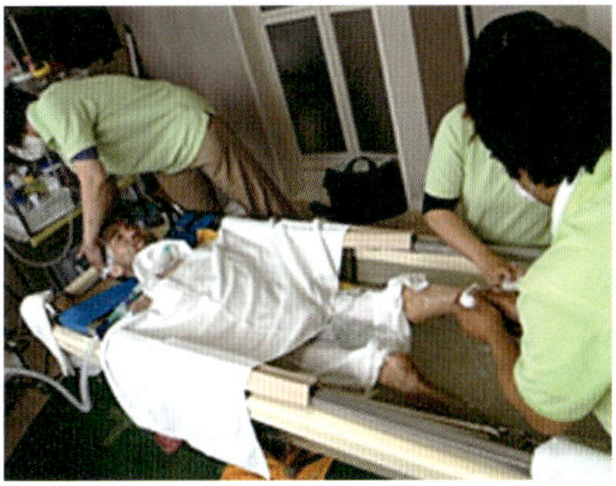

恐怖

いっぱい話すと、疲れて、
舌と口が思うように動かなくなってきた。

徐々に顔に来てる……。
声を取られてから３か月で、もう口パクもか。
どうやって戦えばいいかわかんない相手、
どう倒せばいいんだよ。チクショー。

目しか動かなくなる恐怖。
目も動かなくなる恐怖。
今朝も目が覚め、その先の状態を考えてしまい、パニック。

自殺の思いに襲われ続けながら、自分を落ち着かせた。

希望と絶望って、ホントに隣合わせ。

Fear

I noticed that when I speak too much my face gets tired and my tongue and mouth stops moving the way I want it to. It's slowly coming to my face.
It's only been 3 months since I lost my voice.
How am I supposed to beat something I can't fight? Dammit!
Fear of only being able to move my eyes...
Fear of not even being able to move my eyes...
Woke up again in the middle of the night to this possibility, and panicked.
Thoughts of killing myself overwhelmed me but was able to calm down...
Hope and despair... they go hand-in-hand.

気づいた……

「あなたはしゃべれるからって、しゃべりすぎ」
不必要な言葉が多い。

「あなたは動けるからって、動きすぎ」
不快感を感じるのが早すぎる体。

「あなたは食べすぎ、飲みすぎ、快感を求めすぎ、
そして文句言いすぎ」

俺もそうできるのが楽しみ。

それが「生きる」だからね。

I notice...
"You talk too much... because you can."
Too many unnecessary words.
"You move too much... because you can."
Because your bodies are too quick to find discomfort.
"You eat too much, drink too much, and pleasure yourself too much and then complain too much"
I can't wait to do the same because that's living.

選択

また迷う。
尿道カテーテルをつけっぱなしにするか、
今の使える機能を保とうとしながら、危ないときだけ頼るか。

この間は、1リットルおしっこが溜まった。
痛みで目まいがして、気絶しそうだった。
それが今年、もう何回かおきてる。

あの破裂しそうな痛み。腎臓にも悪いらしい。
チューブ入れたり出したりするのも、
いちいち0.2秒ほど気を失う「特別」な痛み。
もうイヤだ。

けど普段は大丈夫なんだよ。
だからなかなか、チューブをもう一本、体に永久的につけるのを
受け入れられない……。

けどつけたほうが安全。

けど……。
チックショー。

Choice

I'm stuck again. Put in an urethral catheter and keep it in forever or try to keep peeing on my own, and depend on a catheter only on emergencies.
The last time, I held and pissed a liter. It hurt so much that I got dizzy and almost fainted.
This has happened a few times this year already that bursting pain.
It's bad for my kidneys.
Then, there is the pain that makes me unconscious for 0.2 seconds each time the catheter is put in or out...
I've had enough.
BUT it's usually ok you know?
So it's tough letting go, and accepting yet another tube to be stuck in my body...
BUT it is safer to put it in...
BUT...
Dammit.

毎日の夢

朝の儀式（トイレや、身体をふいたり、着替えたり）が終わったら、

決定的瞬間がやってくる。

毎日、ヘルパーがパソコンをベッドに運んでくるまでの
ほんの5〜10秒の間に、

僕は夢をみる。

毎日、考える。
「治療法が見つかったよ！」っていう、
100通のメールや、100個のフェイスブックの投稿があったら
どうしよう、って。

ま・い・に・ち、欠かさず……。

いつかきっと、あなたのメールから、僕の人生は変わるだろう。

Everyday I Dream

Every day, after the morning rituals are done (toilet, wipe down of body, change, etc.),
THE MOMENT OF TRUTH
Every day, for the short 5~10 seconds that it takes for my helper to bring the computer to my bed,
I DREAM.
Every day, I think, what if, I have 100 emails, 100 posts on Facebook, etc. all trying to notify me that a cure has been discovered!
EVERY · SINGLE · DAY...
One day I'm sure, my life will change... from your emails.

オレはまだ生きてる

英語でよく言う、

「死にさえしなければ、その経験はあなたを強くする」

もし、それがホントならば、診断のショックに耐え、
少しずつ全身の動きがなくなる屈辱を冷静に受け止め、
元からある穴から新しい穴まですべてに管を入れられる痛みに耐え、
何度も何時間もキツイ体勢にはまるのに耐え、
死まで数分って状態の経験を２回耐え、意地悪なニヤリに耐え、
などの経験をしたオレが治らないことを、アンタは願うべきかもね。

もし治ったら、幸せになること、強く生きること、
儲けることや、アンタの人生を笑顔で沈めること、
アンタの価値・政策を変えることが、
どんだけ簡単になるかわかってんの？

言葉に気をつけろ。

オレは動いてないけど、100%生きてるのを忘れんな。

I'm still alive

They say, "What won't kill you, will only make you stronger."
If that's true, from handling the shock of the diagnosis, to slowly becoming paralyzed, to taking the pain of the tubes stuck in every hole I have (old & new), to withstanding the hours being stuck in the most uncomfortable positions, to experiencing death being just minutes away... twice, to tolerating the evil smirks etc...
You better hope I don't get better.
Do you understand how easy being happy, being strong, making money, destroying your life with a smile, changing your values/policies will be if I get through this? Do you?
Watch your mouth.
I may not be moving but don't forget, I am still very much alive...

お茶の水中学で講演

母校の道徳の授業で、中2相手に話をした。

起立、礼、「よろしくお願いします!」で、もう泣きそうだった。
なんか強いもんがあって。
「オレが泣いてどうすんだよ」ってこらえた。

僕の中学時代の同級生がプレゼンを読んでくれる間、
生徒を見てみると、興味を持ってくれているのがわかった。
そして、その後ろに座ってる親の方々の何人かは泣いていた。
だけど一番、胸を打たれたのは、生徒たちの目。
誰一人、僕から目をそらさず、話を聞いて、質問をしてくれた。

見て見ぬふり、ジーって見てるくせに
目が合うとそらす大人社会での経験とは、遠く離れていた。

最高の経験、力をもらった。ホント楽しかったです。

Lecture at Ochanomizu Jr. High
So I gave a presentation on "LIVING" to the 8th graders at my former middle school.
It was hard to hold my tears back when they walked in all properly and bowed to start the class. I don't know why but there was something nostalgic or pure. Or maybe I was just being weak. Anyway, the students were into it. Parents were crying.
But what surprised me the most were the students.
When I was just chilling, speaking, or when they asked questions, they looked straight into my eyes. Not one looked away.
A refreshing difference from the now normal double-takes and stares ending with an abrupt avert when our eyes meet.
It was a great experience. It gave me strength, and it was simply fun.

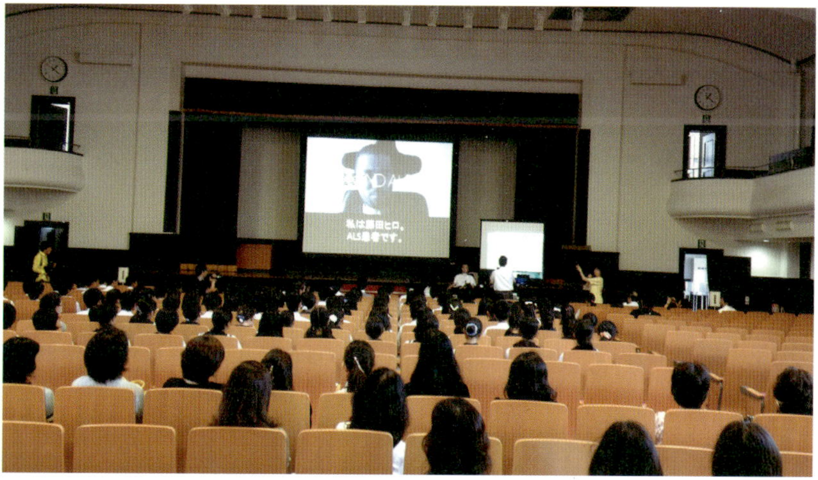

2歳児

どの赤ちゃんも、2歳ぐらいにヒドイ反抗期があるという。
なぜか、火がついたように泣き叫ぶ時期。
大人はわけがわからず、
子どもが落ち着くまで待つしかない。

これは、コミュニケーションの存在を認識したけど、
「どうやって」がわからないから、
イライラでパニックになり、ヒステリーをおこすのだと思う。

これを33歳で経験するとは。
状況は理解している。
けど心で「なんでわかんねーんだよ！」と叫んでいる。

私は2歳児。
落ち着け……。

I am 2

Every baby has their terrible twos.
Crying and screaming hysterically.
Adults not knowing what they want,
Confused, people just wait for the child to calm down.
It's cause the child has learnt about communication but doesn't know how.
That frustration leads to the panic and hysteria. To experience this at 33.
I know what's happening, I do, but it makes me cry out WHY THE FUCK DON'T YOU UNDERSTAND!!
I'm a 2 yr old boy...
Easy...

ある光景

最近なぜか、死にそうになってER（救急救命室）に
連れていかれたときの光景がよく頭をよぎる。

気絶したことはあるが、窒息の経験は初めてだった。
酸素がなくなり、突然汗びっしょりになり、パニック、過呼吸。
すべてがクラクラするなか、周囲の音が山びこのように聞こえ、
徐々に無音になる。
この時点ではおもらしをしている。

ビジュアルがまたすごい。
グーグルアースみたいに超ズームアウトして、銀河系が見えた。
次の瞬間、突然またベッドで窒息している自分に戻る。
その繰り返し。

**すべてが暗く、冷たく、石っぽく、風が吹いてる……。
不快ではなく、ちょっとした心地よさがある。**

考えてみれば、映画「ロード・オブ・ザ・リング」で
指輪をつけるシーンに似てる。

A scene
I get flashbacks a lot these days of the couple times I almost died, and was carried to the ER. I've been knocked out before but nothing like going unconscious from suffocation. Just my experience... You lose air and sweat bullets...then panic about that fact causing you to hyperventilate. Things get dizzy then everything starts to echo... Until it all fades into silence. At this point you're pissing yourself... The visuals are crazy. It's like Google Earth but zooming out to dark space seeing galaxies... Then zooming right back to this life on the bed gasping for air. Back and forth. **Then everything turns black, cold, stone, windy... but not miserable, kind of comfortable...** come to think of it very similar to the visuals when Frodo puts on the ring...

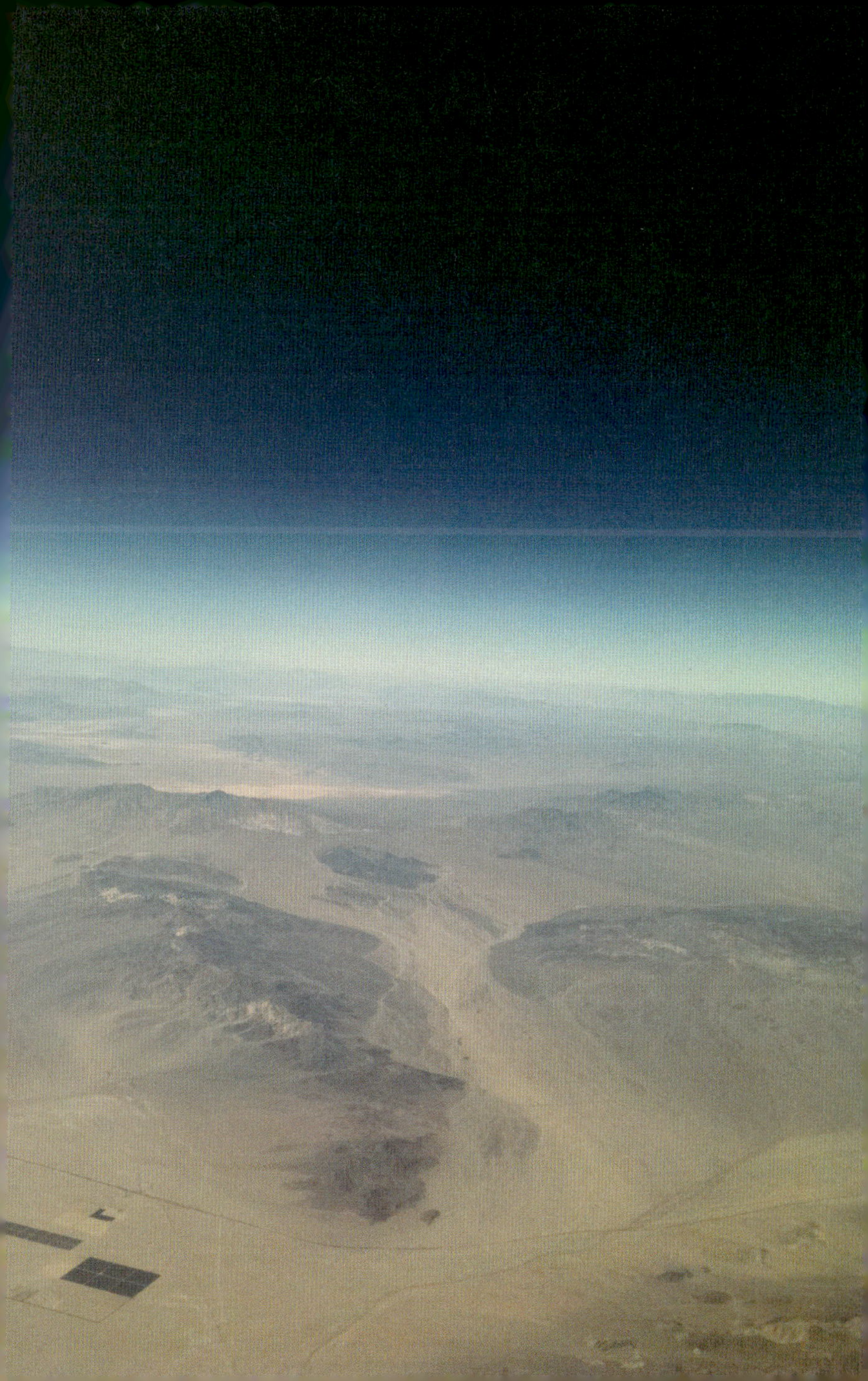

質問

小肌って美味しいんですか？
富士山からの景色は泣けますか？
フジロックってだるくないですか？
ようかんと抹茶ってうまいっすか？
マラソン完走って気持ちいいですか？
マルガリータって物足ります？
スキューバって怖くないですか？
祭りのりんごアメっておいしいですか？

まだまだいろいろ経験したかったなー。
**それも経験しないで
死ぬならまだしも、
経験しないで生きなきゃだからね。
考えてもしょーがないけどね。**

Questions
Do gizzards taste good?
Does the view from Mt. Fuji make you teary eyed?
Doesn't Fuji Rock Festival get tiring?
Does Yokan sweets with Matcha green tea taste good?
Does it feel amazing to finish a marathon?
Are Margaritas good?
Isn't scuba diving scary?
Are those candy apples at festivals good?
There are so many things I wished I had tried.
**To die without experiencing all is one thing.
But having to have to live wondering is a different story.
Well, no use thinking about it now.**

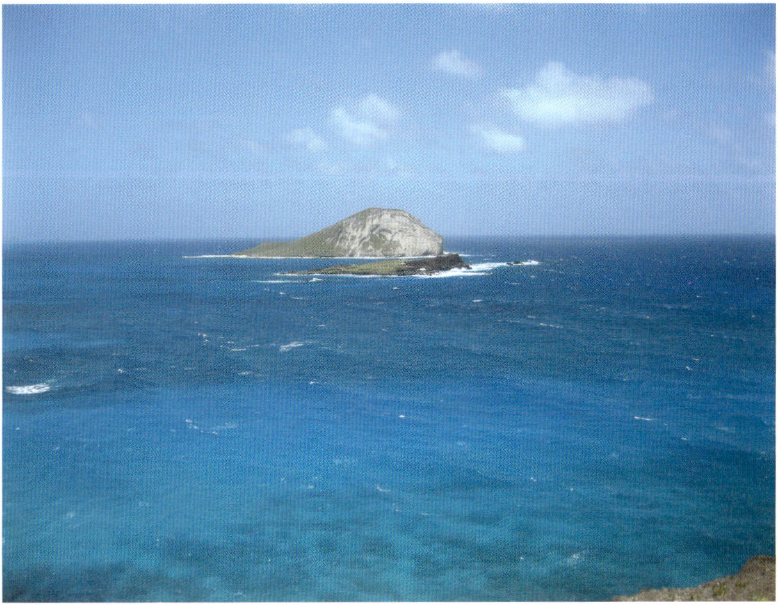

穴

2週間に1回、喉に入ってるカニューレを入れ替える。
この痛みは、ホント説明しにくい。
固形のモノを吐き、それをそのまま、また喉に押し込まれる感じ?
とにかく楽しい時間です。

穴、意外と大きいでしょ。

Hole

Every 2 weeks, my tracheotomy tube is exchanged for a new one.
This is another painful process that's hard to explain.
Imagine vomiting solids, then pushing those solids back into your throat.
It's a wonderful experience.
The hole's pretty big right?

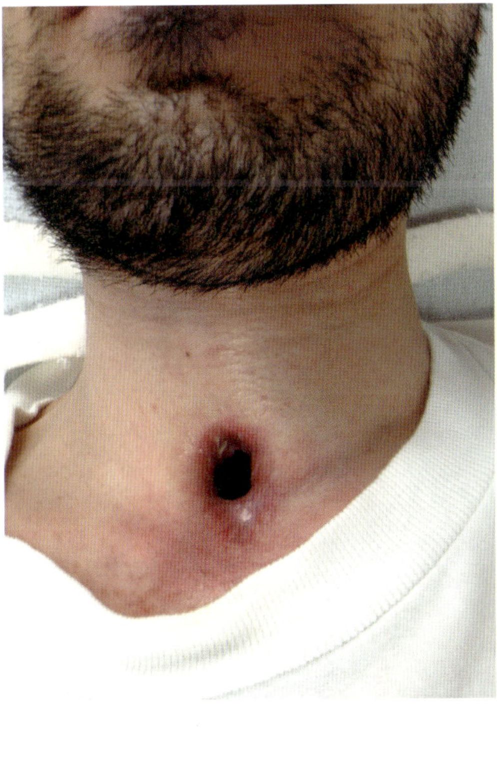

一秒も休んでない

人に一番伝えにくい、わかってもらいにくいことは
「毎秒」闘っているということ。

休憩とか、リフレッシュとか、一服とか、
「ほっ」とする瞬間がほぼない。

映画を見たりとか、
安定剤を飲んでどうにか現実逃避ができても、
「ほっ」とは３年間してない。

毎日神経が張っている。
毎秒。

それを僕よりはるかに長い時間、家族、友達もいないまま、
10年、20年と耐えてる方たちもいる。

そのうえ、目も動かなくなった方々もいる。
毎秒、狂わないように脳のなかでなにを行っているのだろうか。
ゲーム？　思い出を振り返ってる？

想像できない。
一秒でも早く解放を……。

Not 1 second

What's most difficult to explain and for people to understand is that my fight is constant.
It's every second.
There is not a moment to relax or refresh or let out a sigh of relief.
I can escape reality by watching a film or taking some pills but I haven't felt any "relief" for three years.
I'm tense, every second of every day.
There are people who've been enduring this state for 10, 20 years, without any family or friends.
On top of that, some have lost the movement in their eyes.
What are they doing, inside their head, to keep sane, every second?
A game? Or walks down memory lane?
I can't imagine what it's like.
Free us... even if it's a second earlier.

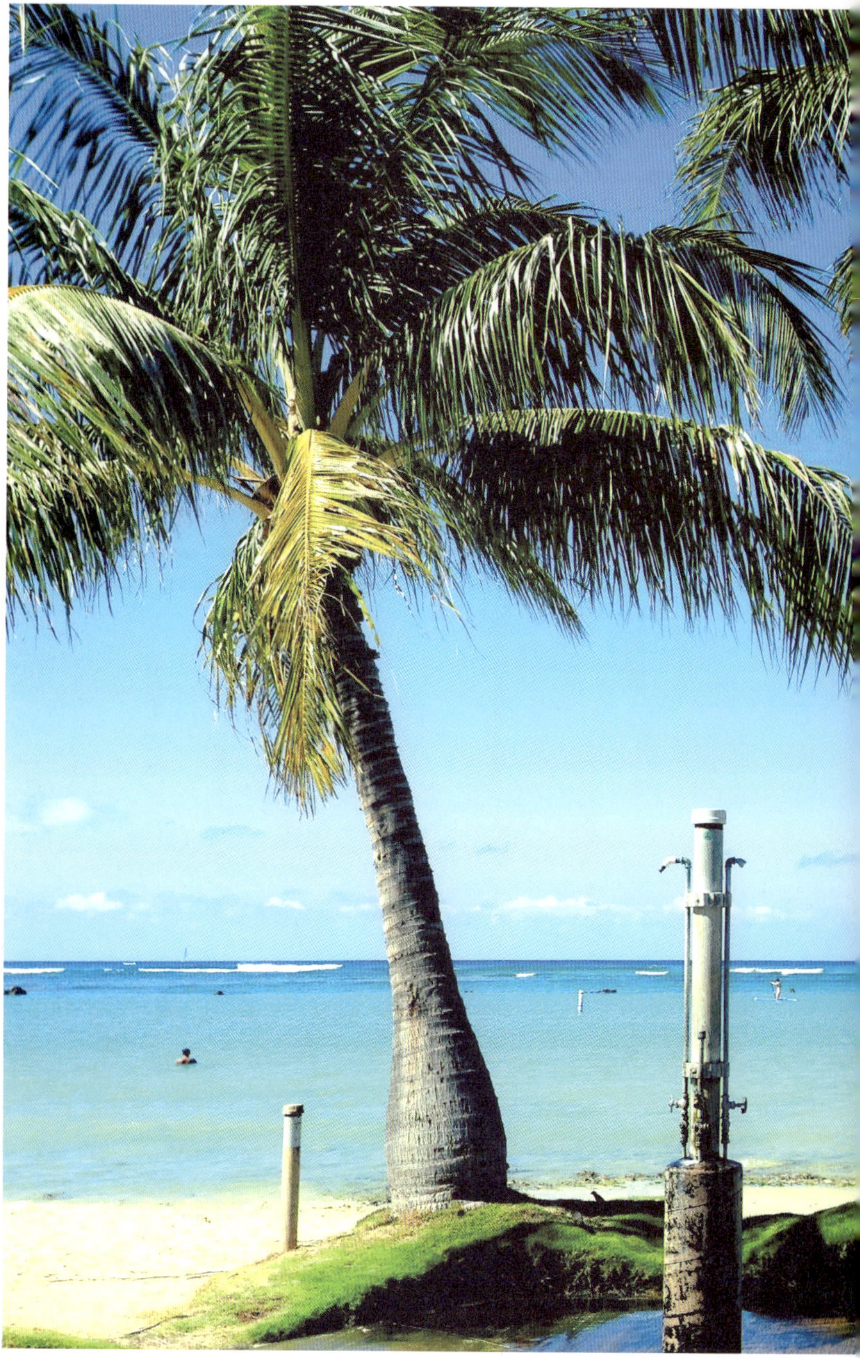

感謝

たぶん皆は、僕がコーラ、ビール、ジュースとか、
ピザ、寿司、ハンバーガーを口にしたがっていると
思っているだろう。

けど、一番欲してるのは、普通の水。冷たいお水だ。
それだけ。

飾りがあるのもいいが、
やっぱり本質には勝てない。

Appreciate

You all probably think I crave coke, beer,
and juice, or pizza, sushi, hamburgers...
But what I wish for THE MOST is a simple cold glass of water...
that's it.

**Decorations are always great but
you can't beat the essentials.**

600通以上の応援

ブログを始めてから、会ったことのない人たちから、
応援メール、手紙、絵、ぬいぐるみ、などを600通以上いただいた。

信じられない……。

僕も目の前で困ってる人がいれば助けるほうだったけど、
知らない人に応援の手紙なんて書こうと思ったことはない。

今まで人の心の温かさを信用できなかった自分が恥ずかしい。
人の愛、温かさって、ホントに捨てたもんじゃない。
すべてのメールを読んでもらいたいぐらい。
個人的な内容も含まれているので、ここで紹介することは
できないけど、とにかくすごいパワーです。

人間に生まれてよかった。

600+ mails of support
Since I started this blog, I've received letters, emails, pictures, stuffed animals, etc. from well over 600 people... that I've never met. It's unbelievable... I was always the one to help out if I saw someone in need but had never even thought of writing a letter of support to someone I've never met. It's embarrassing that I wasn't able to appreciate/trust the kindness of people before. People's love and warmth is amazing. I wish I could share with all of you the words I've received to date. There are some personal things so I can't disclose them but the power/strength behind these words of support is incredible.
I'm glad to have been born human.

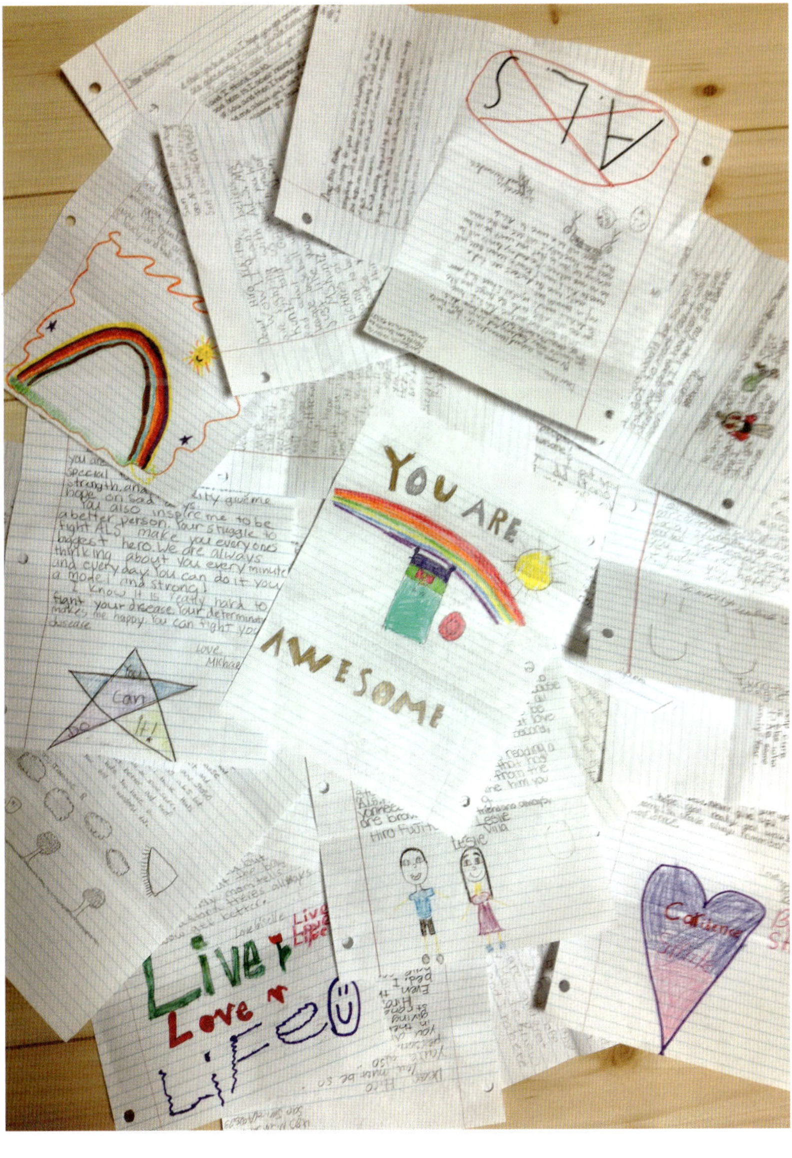

ALS
YOU ARE
AWESOME
You
Can
Do
It!
Live
Love
Life

闘い

常に死にたいと思う、そして生きたいとも思う。

その繰り返し。
それが闘い。

The Battle
I constantly have the desire to die, then the desire to live.
**It's an eternal cycle.
And that's the battle.**

置いていかれる気持ち

俺がこのクソつまんねえ病気とじゃれ合ってる間に、
友人たちは次々と結婚、子どもが生まれ、異国へ移住、
仕事では転職から昇格、もちろん不幸なこともあるけど、
いろいろな経験をしている。

一緒にそれらを経験したかった。
完全に取り残された。傍観者みたい。
今や、コンビニで何が売られているかも知らない。
生死と闘っているんだから、しょうがないことだけど……。

「やべぇ、毎日、遅れてる」と、焦ってる自分がいる。

Feeling left behind

While I'm flirting with this disease, my friends are getting married, having kids, moving abroad, changing jobs, getting promoted. Some have misfortunes along the way too but all-in-all, they are going through new experiences.
I just wish I could've experienced them together.
Sometimes, I feel like an outsider, completely left behind.
I don't even know what's being sold at convenience stores these days and yes, I am fighting for my life, so I guess it can't be helped...but there's an impatient part of me feeling "Damn, I'm getting left behind every day."

何のため

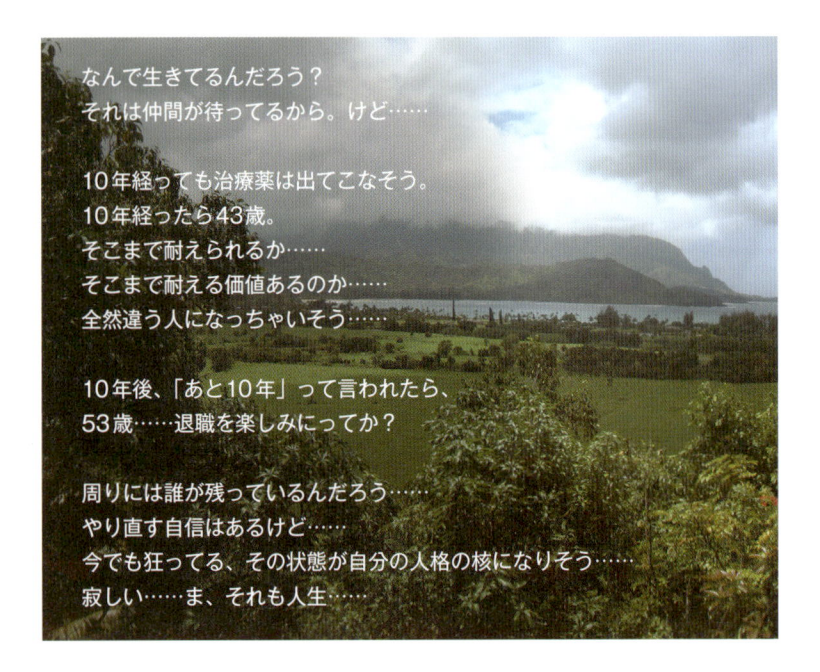

なんで生きてるんだろう？
それは仲間が待ってるから。けど……

10年経っても治療薬は出てこなそう。
10年経ったら43歳。
そこまで耐えられるか……
そこまで耐える価値あるのか……
全然違う人になっちゃいそう……

10年後、「あと10年」って言われたら、
53歳……退職を楽しみにってか？

周りには誰が残っているんだろう……
やり直す自信はあるけど……
今でも狂ってる、その状態が自分の人格の核になりそう……
寂しい……ま、それも人生……

For what?

Why am I living?
Cause my friends are waiting. But...
It doesn't look like there'll be a cure even ten years down the line...
In ten years, I'll be 43.
Can I hold on until then?
Is it worth it?
I will be a completely different person.
What if they say, "in ten years" in ten years, then I'll be 53... by then what, look forward to retirement?
I wonder who'll still be left around me.
I have the confidence to come back again.
But I feel like this craziness/insanity I feel at times may become the core of my personality.
That's sad. But then, I guess that's life too.

どっち

俺が生きてたら親は死んでも死にきれないでしょ。

だけど「親より先に死ぬのは一番の親不孝だ」って言われて育った。

どっちがいいんだよ……。

What am I to do?
If I stay alive like this, how can my parents die in peace?
But they raised me saying "The worst thing for a parent is to bury their child."
So, what am I to do?

僕は最高の「周り」に恵まれてる

天使のような甥っ子を含む、僕を支えてくれる家族。
さまざまな友達の輪、そして、
また彼らが呼ぶ巨大な仲間の輪。

一緒に目標に向かっている会社の戦士達。
最先端の医療チーム。
ネットを通じて出会った励ましや勇気……。

それなのになぜか孤独。
一人で戦ってるとは思わないけど、
ガラスの棺桶に向かってるのは自分一人。

周りに対してはメチャクチャありがたく思ってる。
けど一人の独房で、ずっと独り言が待っているのは間違いない……。

I am blessed with the best surroundings

My family who's behind me 100%, including my angel of a nephew. Various circles of friends, and the gigantic circle of friends surrounding them.
The company comrades all supporting the same mission.
The team of experts at the cutting edge of medicine.
The encouragement, courage, strength delivered through the Internet.
But somehow I feel so, alone...
I would never say that I'm fighting this alone but there's only one glass coffin waiting and it's for me.
I am completely indebted to those around me.
But it is a fact that the only thing waiting for me is solitary confinement with endless conversations with myself...

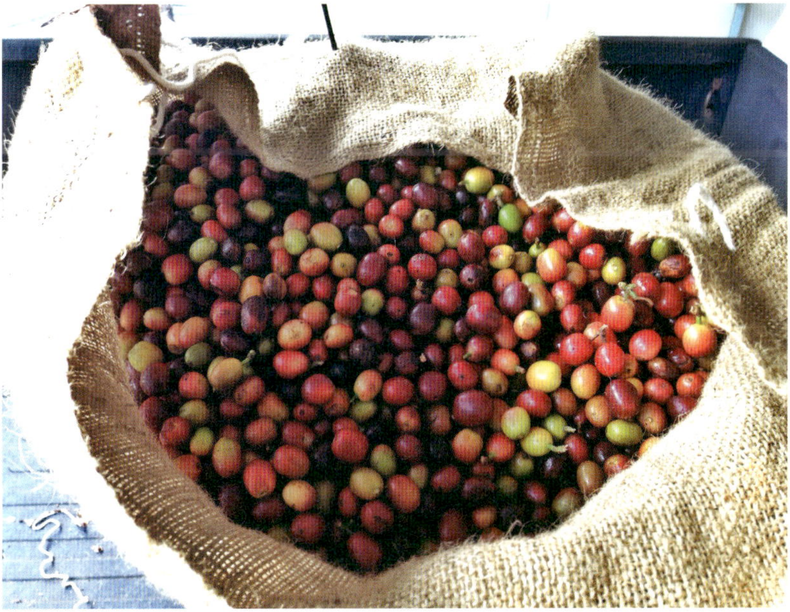

まだまだやることがある

体が弱くなっていくのを感じる。
スタミナ、顔の筋肉、全体的な元気。
どんどん衰えているのがわかる。

だけど、いつもALS完治後の生活を妄想してる。
一晩中語りたい人が多すぎ。やること多すぎ。
絶対勝たないといけない戦いが、まだまだ多すぎ。

絶対戻んないと。

単なる夢で
終わらせないでくれ。

頼む……。

I still have a lot to do...

I can feel my body getting weaker...
Stamina, facial muscle, the energy as a whole...
Shit, I'm deteriorating. I feel it...
But somehow I keep daydreaming of life, post-ALS.
So many people I want to speak to all night, without any worries.
So many things to do, and so many fights to win.
I gotta comeback...
Please don't let this finish as a dream.
Please...

甥っこ

４歳の甥っ子が来た。
お盆だからと、２階にある仏壇に向かった。
小さい手を合わせて「ヒロが早く治りますように」と言ったらしい。
その後、１階にいる自分に、

「かみしゃまが、ヒロもうすぐ治るって言ってたよ」

と……。
嬉しくて、悔しくて、涙が止まらなかった。

そしたら「あっ、ヒロ泣いてる」だって……。

オメーのせいだよ。

いつも、オマエのそばにいるからな……。

Nephew

My 4 year old nephew came over.
He went upstairs to our family altar to pray, cuz it's "Obon," an ancestral holiday in Japan.
He put his little hands together and apparently said "Please let Hiro get better"...
Then he came downstairs to me, "Mr God said you're going to get better soon"...
I was so happy and so... angry, that tears overflowed and kept pouring...
Then he goes "Ah, Hiro's crying"...
It's your fault, you punkass...

I'm always behind you buddy.

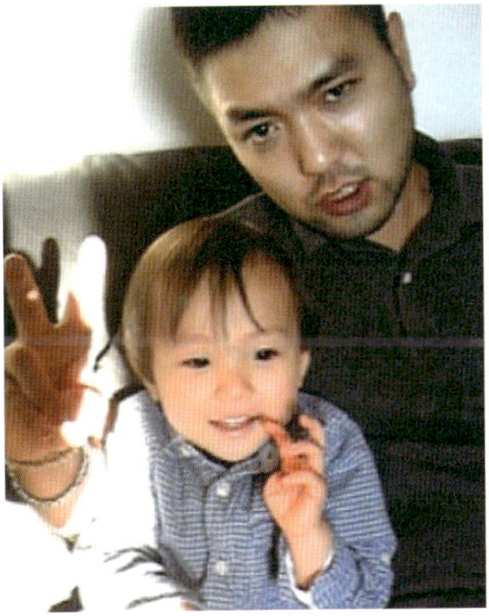

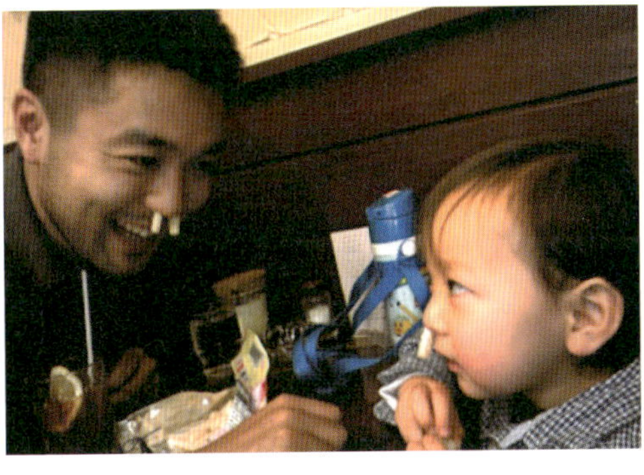

生きて

もしALSを発症する前の自分に問いかけることができたら、なんと言うだろう？

僕は、「どこかへ行く計画を立てるのではなく、今日、富士山に登る、公園で散歩を楽しむ、車で行きたい方向へとにかく走る」と言ったでしょう。

最近、友達が僕のことを知って、自分自身が友達や家族と充分な時間を過ごしているのか、考えるようになったそうです。おそらく誰もがごく自然に考えることでしょうし、僕自身も同じことを考えます。ALSを発症してからは、今まであまり考えなかったことに対して、新たに感謝の念を抱くようになりました。

そこで僕は、「今、自分のいる世界」と充分な時間を過ごしているかどうかを自分に問いかけてみて欲しい、と友達に伝えました。思うがままに、風や芝生や太陽に身を任せているだろうか？ すべての出来事は、この世からの贈り物・プレゼントなのです。一瞬立ち止まって、その素晴らしさを実感する時間をとるかどうかは、自分自身の選択です。僕は、もっと大事なやるべきことがあると思って、今まではこういった瞬間を足早に通り過ぎてきました。それを思うと心が痛みます。

毎朝、ヘルパーさんが自宅を訪れ、一緒にストレッチをしてくれます。彼が窓を開けると、ストレッチをしている間、鳥の鳴き声、車が通り過ぎる音、通学している子どもの声、洗濯物を干している音などが聞こえてきます。今まではそれらをすべて「騒音」として捉えていました。でも今は、この「音」がもっと大きな意味を持っていることに気づきました。

音は動きを表わしているのです。人や物が動いている音、しかし、今の自分はもうほとんど動くことができません。ALSがそれを奪っていくのです。

こうなることがわかっていたら、もっと周りの世界を感じ、見て、呼吸して、感謝の気持ちを持って過ごしていたと思います。だから皆さんは、明日公園で散歩をして、その楽しさを味わってください。

そして、僕を探してみてください。きっと笑顔で散歩する僕がいるはずです。

LIVE

If I could have talked to Hiro before he developed ALS, what would I have said to him?
I would have said: go climb Mount Fuji today, enjoy regular walks in the park, rent a car and drive absolutely anywhere, rather than always planning to go somewhere.
A friend recently said that my situation made him wonder whether he was spending enough quality time with his friends and family. It's a natural thought process, and certainly one that I experience as well. ALS has brought me a new appreciation for things to which I had not given much thought before. So, I asked my friend to ask himself whether he was spending enough quality time with "the world."
Are we spending enough time being carefree, surrendering to the wind, the grass and the sun? Everything we encounter is like a presentation from the world. It's our choice to stop and take a moment to admire it all. It hurts to realize that in the past, I raced through those moments, thinking I had something better to do.
Every morning, my helper comes to my apartment and helps me stretch out. He opens the windows, and while I am stretching, I can hear birds singing, cars driving by, kids playing on their way to school, people doing their laundry and such things.
In the past, I simply brushed this away as "noise." But now, these "noises" mean something more. They represent movement — people and things moving — and movement is something I no longer have. ALS is taking that away from me.
If I had known what was to happen, I would have spent a lot more time feeling, seeing, inhaling and appreciating the world around me. So, I ask you to take a moment tomorrow to walk through the park and simply enjoy it. Look out for me; I'll be the guy taking a stroll, smiling.

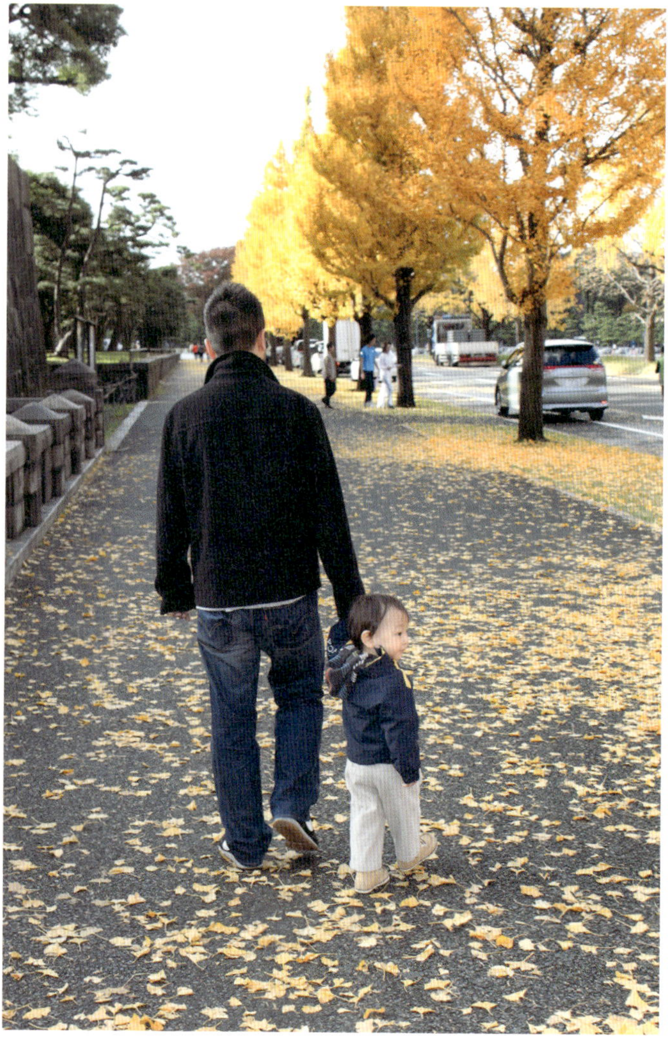

つづく…

To be continued…

おわりに　Acknowledgements

「ありがとう」の連鎖

この本を作るのに手を貸してくださった方々……。

ALSという診断結果に悔しさや怒りを共に感じ、病気の事実を受け入れなかったAd Hoc Inc.のモトイ、有喜。その思いを心から感じてくれたhoneyee.comの鈴木さん。状況をブログで伝える必然性・危機感を理解してくれたクレアクトの下り藤さん。ブログを読んで、その内容を知的に伝える必要性を感じてくれたNHKの木内さん。それらを見て、葛藤のストーリーをより多くの人に知ってほしいと思ってくれたポプラ社の斉藤さん。私の目標達成のために、この貴重な機会を掴みとってくれたMcCann Worldgroupの大木さんをはじめ、内容のアドバイスや写真を提供してくれた同僚や友人、伊東さん、津田さん、青山さん、白水さん、吉村さん、さくら、松浦、Mike、Catherine、Steve、Ross、Kuma、Ami……。

と同時に、雑に聞こえるかもしれませんが、ぜひここに記しておきたいのは、この本を「可能にしてくれた」のは、今まで繋がってきたすべての方々だと心底感じています。思い出を「提供」してくれた家族、仲間、世界……感謝の気持ちでいっぱいです。

名前（知らない名前も）を挙げていくと永遠に続きます。
皆様一人一人に頭が上がりません。

世界中の、心を許す友人たちの上を向いている笑顔。
自らが障害者ながら、僕が開いたALSのイベントに来てくださり、毎月1000円を寄付してくださる方の思いの重み。

会社を訪れる時、いつも「うん」とうなずきながら、エレベーターのドアを開けておいてくれる、70歳近いビル清掃員の方の、笑顔の奥に感じる人生経験の深さ。
すべて今の自分の置かれた立場と照らし合せ、日々勉強、精進させていただいております。
感謝を超えて、罪悪感を超えて、勝手に皆さんを「家族」だと感じています。

正直、今後どのような結果になるかわかりません。
しかし、多くの皆様の貴重な応援をいただいている時点で、私はもうすでに勝ちました。勝利者です。闘病は単なる背景です。
心から、ありがとうございました。

これからも、「皆様との乾杯」に向けて「死ぬ気」で頑張ります。

2013年10月　自宅にて　藤田正裕

Acknowledgements
The chain of "Thank you"

To those who helped create this book...

Motoi and Yuki of Ad Hoc Inc who shared my frustration and anger, and did not accept the facts of ALS. Suzuki-san of honeyee.com who earnestly felt our pain and provided me a stage to share it. Sagarifuji-san of Creact who understood the sense of urgency of getting my voice heard thru that blog. Kiuchi-san of NHK who read my blog and felt the need to communicate it to the mass. Saito-san of Poplar Publishing who saw the TV program and wanted more people to understand the drama surrounding me and ALS. Ohki-san of McCann Worldgroup who saw this precious opportunity to help achieve my goal. Friends and colleagues who provided advise and photos for the content including Ito-san, Tsuda-san, Aoyama-san, Shiramizu-san, Yoshimura-san, Sakura, Matsuura, Mike, Catherine, Steve, Ross, Kuma, Ami.
And at the same time, this may sound general but I truly believe that this book was made possible thanks to every person that I have ever connected with. My family, friends, and the world, who created all of these memories and more. I am forever grateful.
If I list all the names (including those names I don't know) it would go on eternally. I owe it to every one of you.
All of the supportive smiles from my soul-mates around the world. The weight of the 1000 yen donated every month, from the guy who came to one of my events, despite his own disability. The depth of life-experience, behind the 70 some-year-old janitor's smile and nod, who always keeps the elevator door open for me at work.
It all teaches and helps me to grow and move forward.
My feeling has gone beyond gratitude, beyond guilt, and now, just simply consider you all, family.
I have no idea what will happen. However, with all the precious support from so many people, I can say that I have already won. I am the winner. The disease is just the background.

Thank you, from the bottom of my heart. I will continue my fight to the death, in hopes to raise a glass with you all someday soon.

Hiro Fujita　　October 2013 @ home

藤田正裕（ふじた・まさひろ）

1979年11月30日東京生まれ。愛称はヒロ。
幼少期は父親の仕事の関係でアメリカ、スイス、イギリスなどで過ごす。日本に帰国し国立の中学校に転入、高校は東京のアメリカンスクール、大学はハワイに進学した。ハワイのシェラトンホテルでコンシェルジュを務めた後、2004年に日本に帰国し、国際広告会社㈱マッキャンエリクソンに入社。同社でプランニングディレクターとして活躍していた2010年11月、難病である筋萎縮性側索硬化症（ALS）と診断される。現在は、顔と左手の人差し指しか動かない。2013年1月には気管切開し声を失いながらも、視線とまばたきで操作するパソコンのアイトラッキングシステムを使用し、週一出社と在宅勤務で仕事を続けている。また、難病ALSの認知を高め、治療法の確立、そして、患者のコミュニケーションにまつわる医療政策の改革を訴えるため一般社団法人END ALSを立ち上げ、ブログ等を含むメディアを通じてメッセージを発信し続けている。
http://end-als.com
http://blog.honeyee.com/hfujita/
https://www.facebook.com/endalswithhiro

99％ありがとう
ALSにも奪えないもの

2013年11月20日　第1刷発行

著者　藤田正裕
発行者　坂井宏先
編集　斉藤尚美・福丸玲
発行所　株式会社　ポプラ社
〒160-8565　東京都新宿区大京町22-1
電話　03-3357-2212（営業）
　　　03-3357-2305（編集）
　　　0120-666-553（お客様相談室）
FAX　03-3359-2359（ご注文）
振替　00140-3-149271
ホームページ　http://www.poplarbeech.com/

印刷・製本　共同印刷株式会社

ⓒ Masahiro Fujita 2013 Printed in Japan
N.D.C.916/207P/19cm　ISBN978-4-591-13681-2
落丁本・乱丁本は送料小社負担でお取り替えいたします。
ご面倒でも小社お客様相談室宛にご連絡ください。
受付時間は月〜金曜日、9:00〜17:00（ただし祝祭日は除く）。
読者の皆様からのお便りをお待ちしております。
いただいたお便りは編集局から著者にお渡しいたします。
本書のコピー、スキャン、デジタル化等の無断複製は著作権法上での
例外を除き禁じられています。
本書を代行業者等の第三者に依頼してスキャンやデジタル化することは、
たとえ個人や家庭内での利用であっても著作権法上認められておりません。